Plantation Boy

GENEALOGY

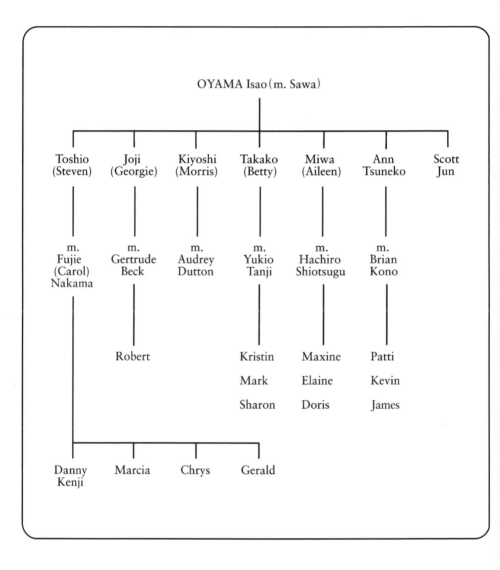

PLANTATION
BOY

Milton Murayama

 University of Hawai'i Press · Honolulu

Printed in the United States of America

03 02 01 00 99 98   5 4 3 2 1

"Let's Go for Broke," words and music by Harry Owens,
© 1935 by Harry Owens.

Library of Congress Cataloging-in-Publication Data
Murayama, Milton.
   Plantation boy / by Milton Murayama.
      p.   cm.
   ISBN 0-8248-1965-9 (cloth : alk. paper). — ISBN 0-8248-2007-X
(paper : alk. paper)
   1. Japanese Americans—Hawaii—Fiction.   I. Title.
PS3563.U723P58   1998
813'.54—dc21   97-33350
                                                              CIP

University of Hawai'i Press books are printed on acid-free paper and meet the
guidelines for permanence and durability of the Council on Library Resources

Designed by Jennifer Lum

FOR THE FAMILY

I

1941-1945

1

Pearl Harbor

The draft called 4 guys from Kahana in 1940. In '41 they call 7 of us, including my girlfriend's brother, Seiji, the Arisumi brothers, Kazu and Toru, and Happy Sumida of Honokawai.

"I'd just as soon get it over with," Happy says.

It shocks me when I flunk the physical. I never knew I had a busted eardrum. *No wonder I was always turning to my right side to hear better!*

"Hey, you lucky buggah!" the guys say.

"Hey, you one boxer too, how come you no wen get one busted eardrum?" they kid Happy.

Was not boxing, was my old man, I was going to say, but let it pass.

Right off the bat I miss Happy. He used to run the 3/4 mile up the hill from Honokawai every day and we'd spar 6–7 rounds. I needed to build up my stamina if I was going to turn pro. After Danny Lowe and I won the Maui lightweight and flyweight championships for the second time in 1939, the plantation built a small gym in the park below the plantation store, and they consolidated Kahana A.C. and Pepelau A.C. into Frontier Mill Athletic Club, and appointed Warren Prescott and Alan Freeland as comanagers. Prescott was the assistant manager of the plantation store on Front Street in Pepelau and Alan owned the Frontier Theatre. Alan also managed the Pepelau Tigers, the barrelweight (over 140 lbs.) barefoot football team.

Then KABOOM! The dumb Bulaheads bomb Pearl Harbor! Over 20 ships sunk, over 2,300 killed! *Assholes! They one flyweight taking on one heavyweight!*

Mr. Hamaguchi gets pulled in. He works for the Japanese consulate in Honolulu. Papa did the same thing when we lived in Pepelau. He reported the births and deaths of the Japanese in Pepelau so that they could be recorded in the family registers in Japan. He got paid only $3 a month, but the old man, he did it for prestige.

All the priests and teachers at the Buddhist language schools and many of the fishermen get snatched in the night by the FBI.

"Get Papa's things ready," I tell Mama.

They came for Mr. Hamaguchi in the middle of the night and he couldn't even pack his toothbrush.

The first week goes by, then the second. *They not coming,* I think. Then on the third Sunday the big new car stops in front of the house and a crew-cut haole and his nisei or *kibei* interpreter in khaki step out. The haole is suntanned and wears an aloha shirt. The guy's a *kamaaina,* an old timer.

"I'd like to speak to Isao Oyama," he says, and the interpreter says it in Japanese.

"Hai." Papa bows and bows like one flunky in a samurai movie.

They go to the lawn next to the pigpens, where I used to spar with Joji and Kiyo. Me and Danny were going to turn pro next year, but that's all *pau.* Martial law says no more than 3 Japanese can congregate.

We all stand near the veranda and watch them. Papa keeps sucking his breath and bowing. Then suddenly he's standing straight and flicking his hand over his head.

What he saying? I move closer, turning my good right ear toward them.

"You had a large boat," the haole says, and the *kibei* translates.

"Tharty-tsu feeto, one hossu power, four knotsu," he brags, holding up four fingers.

"You went out into the open sea?"

"Huh?"

The interpreter translates.

"No can! No can!" Papa yells in pidgin.

"Why not?"

"Naze?"

"Bumbye, no come backu! Onry *holoholo,* no more gasu, no more compassu, loosu, loosu! *Maké, maké!"* He stops flailing and says in an even voice to the interpreter, "I'd drift away and get lost if I went out of sight of land. None of us carried compasses. We found our fishing holes by landmarks. Nobody could find you if you ran out of gas and your anchor rope broke and you drifted away. Two fishermen never made it back." He turns to the haole, "All *maké*."

The haole asks him another question, and Papa looks at the interpreter, who translates: he took out $7,000 in the Kahana Japanese Club account from the Bank of Hawaii in Pepelau in late November. Why?

"No can? No can? Why no stoppu if no can?" Papa says and explains to the interpreter: he read in the papers the assets of Japanese clubs were going to be frozen.

"Where money now?" the haole asks.

"I bringu homu. Keepu insai chicken hausu. I asku Takeshi Tsuda, nisei memba, put undah his namu. Decembah sebun, in chicken hausu. I talku memba, five," holding up 5 fingers, "hundredo dolla, gibu Redo Crossu, okay? Okay. So gibu Redo Crossu five hundredo dolla."

"What happened to the sixty-five hundred?"

"Gibu backu membas. Oba tharty year. Ebery monsu, quarter. Now onry ninety membas. Before tree hundredo membas. Before quarter. Now one dolla...."

The old man enjoyed being president of the Kahana Japanese Club. He talks on and on.

"Are your sons Japanese citizens?" the haole finally asks.

"I wrote the Japanese consulate to cancel their citizenship two years ago," Papa says in Japanese.

"Do you have the record of that?" the haole asks.

"*Oi!*" Papa says and runs past us into the house and brings out the fat envelope from the *tansu*. He gives it to the FBI man.

"Okay, papa-san." The haole laughs.

"Dumb ass!" I tell Kiyo. "He care more for the Japanese Club than us!"

I shake a finger in Papa's face. "You lucky I told you to cancel our dual citizenship."

It's curfew and total blackout. Martial law freezes us to the plantation. No raises. Anybody leaving ends up in Provost Court with a $200 fine or 2 months in jail or both. We exchange our paper money for those with "HAWAII" in block letters printed on the back. Food is rationed and hard liquor is a fifth per month, gasoline 10 gallons per month.

The Japanese capture Singapore, Malaysia, Hong Kong, and the Philippines. The Univ. of Hawaii ROTC students were called into the Hawaii Territorial Guard on December 7, but on January 21 they discharge all the niseis. All kinds of rumors in the air: there were arrows cut into the canefields pointing to Pearl Harbor; one Japanese aviator shot down wore a McKinley High School ring; the Japanese landed in Kahului and were marching over the *pali* road. . . .

Univ. of Hawaii reopens and soon afterward 160 of the nisei students form the Varsity Victory Volunteers to dig ditches and whatnot for the Army. Happy Sumida, Seiji Nakama, and all the niseis in Hawaii National Guard regiments are segregated, their rifles taken away, and detailed to stringing barbwire on the beaches. Niseis are reclassified 4E, ineligible for the draft.

On the West Coast they start evacuating the 110,000 Japanese, of whom 75,000 are American citizens.

"They going send us to Molokai," people keep saying.

"No can," I tell them. "The plantation collapse without Japanee labor. Carlyle going fight tooth and nail to keep us. Besides, the Japanee in Hawaii don't have a pot to piss in. The mainland Japanee, they own land. So even if they chase us out, they come up empty."

I oughta feel lucky, but I don't. My stomach grinds like a washing machine, living with the old farts. I keep yelling at them. How come you keep sending Takako and Miwa to high school!? How much of the debt have we paid!? Takemoto *sensei* says 10 years is all you can ask of me! Filial piety is going to be abolished after Japan loses the war! . . . I live on Alka Seltzer. I take up cigarettes and beer. Boxing is *pau*. I'll be an old man by the time the war's over.

I feel like joining the "drunk pile." They buy a couple cases each of Primo on Saturday after work and drink through the blackout in the park below the plantation store. They sit apart and yell to each other.

"Why you guys no sit closer?" Joe DeMello, the blackout warden, says. "That way you don't hafta yell." He stops by several times a night for free beers.

"The Army wen say 'No more than three Japanee,' "
"Swipe" Yamada says.

The guys sleep on the grass in their work clothes, piss in the hibiscus hedges, and drink and sleep till Sunday afternoon. Then they trudge to the bathhouse to get cleaned up for Monday.

2

Fujie Nakama

Late in '40 I started dating Fujie Nakama. Most high school girls acted haolefied and didn't date us "cane-top college" guys, but then most *naichi* guys didn't go steady with Okinawan girls. The *naichi* parents from the main islands of Japan looked down on the Okinawans, Filipinos, haoles, and everybody else. But my biggest obstacle was Margaret Doi. Fujie and Margaret were like twins. They did everything together—study, bathe, go to dances. Then they graduated at the top of their class of '39. My break came when Fujie went to work at the plantation hospital in Pepelau. The dozen nisei nurse's aides were supervised by one haole registered nurse, and those from out of town boarded at the hospital. I wrote Fujie a note, asking if she'd like to go to the movie at Frontier Theatre some Sunday afternoon. I waited 2 weeks before she replied.

Nothing is secret in Kahana.

The first thing she said was, "What about Kiyoko Kagawa?"

"We broke up."

"You mean she left for Honolulu."

"We broke up before that. She was so slow she used to drive me nuts."

Kiyoko was easy, but it scared me. *What if the rubber leaked and she got* hapai? *We might have a kid like her—a "D" student, or at best a "C."*

Fujie says no sex till marriage. You cannot go into the cane-field in the middle of the afternoon anyway. Besides, all the cane-fields are one good mile away from downtown. It's hard enough for Fujie to get Sunday afternoons off. She has to trade shifts, even take graveyard, which nobody wants.

She's medium pretty, like most of the girls in Kahana. Round face and eyes, button nose, silky skin, and terrific figure. The only real pretty wahine in camp is Chiyoko Komae, and she acts like she shits ice cream.

Then several months after we began dating, Fujie said, "You know what Margaret Doi asked me?"

"What?"

"She asked, 'Why are you going with that garbage collector?'"

It was like a sneak punch. *Why she hate me?* My only comeback was, "How come they no call Kiyo one garbage collector?"

We were both truck-driver helpers and collected the garbage around Kahana when not hauling workers, fertilizer, or cane cuttings.

"He doesn't go around insulting people, that's why," Fujie said.

"I never wen insult Margaret. I wen dance with her only once. She wen pump my arm up and down, up and down. Dan Kondo wen do one fancy dip near us and said, 'Eh, Margaret, how come you pump your hand li'dat?' 'It's not I, it's *he*,' she said, and stopped the pumping. I almost wen shit in my pants!"

"You must've made a pass at her."

"Plain-Jane Margaret!? Caw-mon, give me some credit. I get better taste."

"But people call you *sukebei*."

"Me? Not me. They must mean Joji. He's the ladies' man."

On our first Valentine's Day, I said, imitating the Kahana guys, "You going be my valentine or wat!?"

"You should say, 'Will you be my valentine?'" she said.

"Awwrrrrgh!" I vomited make-believe.

"You Kahana men are so *bobura*. You act like you're back in nineteenth-century Japan."

"Will you be my valentine, eh?"

In the spring of '41 Danny Lowe and I won our respective Maui championships again, and again got beat at the territorial finals in Honolulu. But we were going to turn pro in '42, win or lose.

"Let's get married. I no can stand any more necking," I proposed one day after matinee.

"What will your parents say?"

"I disown them if they say no."

When I asked the old farts, Papa said, "You're too young."

"What about you!? You married at 21! I'm 22! I've already worked six years and we haven't paid back a cent! I'll do it for four more years and it's *pau!*"

"Father worked twelve years for your grandfather," Mama said.

"All right, six more years, but that's it!"

I would've slammed them if they'd objected because she's Okinawan. Fujie and I agreed we'd give them all of Fujie's pay for one year and one-third of mine for 6 years.

Papa asked Mr. Kawai to act as matchmaker for a June wedding.

One Sunday at dusk I walk Fujie back to the hospital. I keep walking Honolua way. About a block past the hospital is the Japanese Methodist Church. It felt so far away when I was in short pants. It has a big yard. Far behind the church are the wood-frame buildings of the language school. It's closed now, maybe forever.

There are no stores, just houses for half a mile, then the stream from Mango Gulch and a short concrete bridge over it. The pineapple cannery, a large corrugated sheet-iron building, is on the right. On left are the Uehara Store, Shishido Restaurant, and the ocean.

"Hey, Tosh!" Joji calls, stepping out of Shishido's.

He works at Baldwin Packers and rooms and boards at Shishido. The guy is lucky. He still has to give most of his pay to the old farts, but he doesn't have to live with them.

"Wachu doing?" he asks.

"Hitching a ride."

"You might as well wait here. They all have to pass here."

"Yeah." I sit on the steps. "Fujie and me, we going get married."

"She *hapai?*"

"Wachu take me for!? I not one of these Kahana guys! Naw, we not going start one family yet. I going take one corre-spondence course. Fujie going help me. There's a job hauling bagasse six P.M. to six A.M. Nobody wants it so I going ask for it. We going live in Pepelau. Shit, I no can study living with the old futts. They drive me nuts."

"The old folks not bad. They angels compared to other parents."

"Yeah, but those other parents no leave the sons with a six-G debt."

"You should look on the bright side. If Papa was successful, we be in Japan and you'd be in the Japan Army."

Rev. Sherman, the Methodist minister, asks the Army to relax the no-more-than-three-Japanese rule and comes to the house to marry us on Saturday, June 6. Fujie's sister, Mariko, who just graduated Pepelau High, is her bridesmaid. Thank God it's not Margaret Doi. Takemoto *sensei* and our matchmaker, Ichiro Kawai, and their wives are the only guests. Fujie looks so serious. *Margaret all wet. I'll prove it to you,* I feel like saying. Our eyes meet and a soft smile spreads across her face. There's no *sake* or beer. Only homemade sushi, *nishime,* and condiments. We talk in whispers almost. Something's in the air. Rumors of battles. Where? Near Hawaii?

I used to think Rev. Sherman was just another nice-guy haole minister who didn't want to rock the plantation boat. But soon after Pearl Harbor he went to the Army and swore everyone in his congregation was loyal. Which is why Papa and Takemoto *sensei* never got pulled in. Then he asked Jack Carlyle to give *sensei* a *hanawai* job, irrigating the canefields. It's strange to see *sensei* so tanned, but he looks tired and thinner.

A month later we get a letter from Seiji, Fujie's brother, from Camp McCoy in Wisconsin. Fourteen hundred fifty-three of them from the 2 Hawaii National Guard battalions volunteer into an all-nisei 100th Infantry Battalion. They'll be trained to fight in Europe.

"You know," I tell Fujie, "they wen ship them out on our wedding day, the day of the Battle of Midway. That's when they started evacuating the West Coast Japanese too. They no trust us."

"You're too suspicious."

I get a surprise letter from Happy.

Congratulations! Fujie's going to be good for you. She's one smart wahine. She made me feel dumb in Latin I & II. Maybe she'll teach you a thing or two. My best wishes to her.

I like stateside, i.e., when I can get out. Things are so different. The haoles here are working class: waitresses, janitors, farmers, day laborers, etc. They're not only tough but also hard working. The plantation haoles are colonists actually, the white man's burden and all that. In fact to the poor Indians I see around here, all America is a colony.

The townspeople treat us pretty nice. Most are third- and fourth-genertion Germans. People used to stone dachshunds in the last war, so they must feel for us. Besides, we've got some things in common. We're both obedient, stoic, and meticulous to a fault.

I was never made for the Army. I go nuts if I can't have some time to myself. So I go to the latrine after lights out to read. So I'm always late for reveille and I get caught with only my long johns under my overcoat. So I'm always peeling potatoes. It's so ████████ spit and polish it's ████████ ████ To bad we don't have a boxing team. It'd be an outlet.

Pals,

"K. P." Happy

"What's 'stoic'?" I ask Fujie.
"To be full of *gaman.*"
"And 'meticulous'?"
"Komakai toko ni ki ga tsuku."
"Yeah, Bulaheads petty buggahs."
Happy always used 2-dollar words and spoke good English, but nobody razzed him or called him "haolefied."

We live with the old farts till my new job comes through. We rent a 2-bedroom woodframe house on Back Street behind the Pepelau Plantation Store for $25. We buy secondhand furniture on credit. Right away my stomach feels better and I cut down on Alka Seltzer.

3

American Correspondence School

I write the American Correspondence School in Chicago as soon as we get settled. When I take their aptitude test, they tell me I should be an artist. "I don't want to starve, I want to make money," I write them. They suggest the next best, architectural drafting.

Working 6:00 P.M. to 6:00 A.M. turns the world upside down. There's a gauze curtain over everything. People's voices sound muffled and my own voice is an echo. Finally, when things settle down, it's time to go to work.

Bagasse is the cane stalk after it's been crushed and ground into fiber. It filters down the chute and fills my truck bed in 35 minutes. I can squeeze in 4 hours of study between 6 and midnight. The round-trip to the dumpsite in Honokawai takes 25 minutes in the blackout. My headlights are covered with blue cellophane and I can see only a few feet ahead of me, but there's no traffic. Then while I wait for the Mack to fill up again, I study in the cab of the truck with the flashlight covered with blue cellophane.

"Hey, Tosh, wachu doin'?" One by one the mill workers ask me.

"I studying algebra."

"How come?"

"I trying to get one drafting diploma."

"Yeah? For what?"

"I don't wanna die on the plantation."

They all give me advice. "You going spoil your eyes"; "The war going last forever"; "Take it easy. You trying too hard. . . ."

If not for Fujie, I think I quit. She had algebra I and plane geometry so she helps me. But I'll be on my own with algebra II, solid geometry, and trig, and they're only the foundation!

"The beginning is the hardest," Fujie says.

Guadalcanal taking so long. At that rate it'll take 10 years. The Japanese no going give up, they going fight island by island. So what's the use? I going get frozen to the bagasse for 10 years. But if I no study now I'll be nothing in 10 years.

"Hey, Tosh, you wasting your time, take it easy," Satoru Kimura says one night.

"You know what? You going die on the plantation like the old futts!"

"Yeah?"

"Yeah!"

"I was just kidding." He shrugs and goes back into the mill.

Kidding, shit! They don't have the guts to come right out. The mill workers act high *maka-maka*, they think they better than the field-workers.

"You're being too sensitive," Fujie says.

"Naw, they don't wanna see anybody get ahead."

One morning I run home after work with a mean hard-on. Fujie starts at 8 so we have time. She's all dressed fixing my breakfast. I kiss her. She giggles and keeps cooking. I try the slow approach. I rub her shoulders, move to the back.

"Don't." She slaps my hand.

"Whassa matter?"

"We don't have time."

"We get one hour."

"I'm having coffee with Margaret Doi."

"You choose Margaret over me!?"

"She's leaving for Honolulu today."

"You know, you and Margaret, you two of a kind. Margaret the president and you the vice president."

"Of what?"

"The Kahana Plain-Jane Club."

"Margaret was right. You're just a garbage collector and a bum."

"She wen call me one bum too?"

"A garbage collector *and* a bum."

"I slap your head!"

"Go ahead, slap my head." She puts down the spatula and turns. "Just because you're a boxer you think you're so hot, eh? Go ahead, hit me." She jigs, sneering like Margaret.

BANG! My right cross shoots out. The rest is slow motion. She flops on the green and white linoleum and staggers up without taking the count. She looks dazed, then glares at me. She beelines for the bedroom. I feel like hell. *But she shouldn't make fun of me like that, jumping up and down, sticking out her chin.* I hear her packing. I turn off the gas. She was fixing my favorite Portuguese sausage, eggs, and potatoes.

"Where you going?" There's no swelling. I aimed for the tip of the chin. She looks straight ahead and walks out. She walks to Front Street and turns right.

Shit, why she no can spare 15 minutes? Or even 10? I work 12 hours, 7 nights, and study, study, study. I cannot stop on a dime. She works only 48 hours. Why she no can give me 10 minutes? I need it to fall asleep. The skin used to be real tender down there, but now it's callused and tight, and it's hard to jack off!

I get so mad I drink one beer after another, but Primo is so weak I cannot get drunk enough to fall asleep. The more I drink the madder I get. *How come I so dumb!?* Like the time I shaved my head working at Aoki Store. Everybody laughed. But when I rode my bicycle to Pump Camp to take orders, I got lots of orders. People buy from you if you can make them laugh. It was so hot that summer I thought it'd be cooler. At least hair grows back. Not foreskin. It was a *papale hemo* day for 3 of us in Filipino camp. The first guy said, "Hit some more, hit some more!" and fainted. There was a small chopping block, a razor, boiling water, and lots of banana leaves. They rubbed the prick with some kind of plant juice to make it numb, but I yelped when he chopped. The bandaged head was the size of a tennis ball for the next 2 months. It bled every time I had a hard-on. *Why I so stupid!?* It was supposed to help my boxing and fucking stamina. *So why she make fun of my boxing? I was the Maui champ 4 out of 5 years! Why she no can lie down and spread her legs for 10 minutes!? Why she no can spare jes' 10 minutes! You can even squeeze a whole boxing match in 11 minutes!*

I'm soused by 5:50 when I walk to the mill with my books and peanut butter/jelly sandwich. I cannot concentrate. All night long I stare at nothing. It's worst about 3. The mill looms up like a giant ship. My Mack is a small launch. I'm all alone with the roar of the crushers. Time crawls.

What if she no come back? Divorce after 6 months? Margaret will crow. I'll quit the correspondence course. She corrects my grammar all the time. "It's haole talk," I say. "Pidgin is plantation talk," she says.

She's not home at 6:15. After 10, I go to Aoki Store and call the hospital. She called in sick. She must be in Kahana. *It's not that bad,* I tell myself. *Think of the guys dying in the Pacific and Europe.*

Then about 3 I hear the screen door open.

"You still mad at me? I dint mean to do it."

She shrugs.

"I sorry I hit you. You shouldn't stick out your chin like that. Especially to one boxer."

"A punch-drunk boxer." She chokes off a giggle.

"Is the way you wen skip, 'Hit me, hit me.' " I jig and flap my elbows to show how silly she looked. "I wen lose control. Sorry, eh?"

"How was Margaret?" I ask later.

"Huh?"

"You were going to have coffee with her."

"Oh, I canceled it."

A couple days later she says her mother told her, "You knew he was a boxer when you married him, so you go back to him." The following week she says she's pregnant.

"*You supposed to use the diaphragm! We cannot afford one kid now!*" I was gonna say, but I hold back. She might not have come back otherwise.

4

Oyama's Pigs

With Fujie's help I finish algebra I and plane geometry in 6 months. I'm on my own with algebra II.

One day Fujie comes home from work and drops a bomb! Both Mama and Miwa are pregnant! *Goddamn old farts! They keep pooping babies and expect us to support them! I told them over and over! Educate the boys! The girls will get married and not pay you back!*

Only last month I saw Miwa having ice cream and soda at the drugstore on Front Street.

I drove my truck up to Kahana and yelled at Mama, "Why do you send Miwa to high school! She's not even good at school! She spends my money for ice cream and soda!"

"It can't be helped," Mama said. "She rides the Tsuda car to school. What's Miwa supposed to do when the others decide to stop for ice cream and soda?'

"Why don't you send her in the Perreira bus!?"

"They both cost five dollars a month."

"So you throw away ten dollars I give you on the girls' carfare! Why do you send the girls to high school!? They'll get married, they'll never pay you back!"

"Canefield girls marry canefield boys, high school girls high school boys," she said.

"You sending them to high school to catch husbands!? What about me, Joji, and Kiyo!?"

"Boys are different."

"I'm washing my hands of you and Papa in three years! Ten years is the limit! Japan is *pau*, filial piety is *pau!*"

"Don't worry, we won't depend on you. We'll depend on Joji and Kiyoshi."

"*Bakatare!* You and Papa came here as plantation workers and you'll die as plantation workers! You haven't raised yourself one inch! Not one inch! You'll die on the plantation!"

"Don't worry, we won't depend on you. There are Joji and Kiyoshi," she said.

"Bakatare!"

All the money we gave them—Fujie's $30 and my $25—was money down the drain! None of the debt was paid off! Ten dollars right off the bat went for the girls' carfare to Pepelau High!

I drive breakneck to dump my first load in Honokawai and rev the Mack up to Kahana and storm into the house in my boots. "How come I'm the last to find out you and Miwa are pregnant!? You said every child must repay his parents! How is Miwa going to repay you!?"

She sits at her sewing machine and guns the motor. "It can't be helped. It's like raising pigs. There's bound to be *kuzu*," she says without looking up.

"So we're pigs now! Oyama pigs! Why didn't you stick to raising pigs!?"

"Don't worry, we won't depend on you. We'll depend on Joji and Kiyoshi . . ."

"Bakatare!"

The next day I dump the first load and drive down Pigpen Avenue kicking up dust. I cannot stand her, but I cannot keep away. I shout and yell, but she comes right back with her smart answers.

"It can't be helped," Fujie says.

"You talking just like the old futts! *Shikata ga aru! Shikata ga aru!*" I yell at *her*.

"But you're only hurting yourself. You have to let go and go on with your life."

"How can I when they get a hook in me!?"

"You have no other choice." She's always so calm.

I'm all alone when she leaves for work. I'm so mad I cannot sleep. I walk to the pineapple cannery a mile away on the west end of town.

It's off-season and most of the machines are idle. Joji is an apprentice to Albert Nakai, the machinist, who was his "trainer" when he fought for Baldwin Packers.

Joji comes over wiping his hands on a rag.

"You know Mama and Miwa pregnant!? Damn old futts, they keep pooping babies and they expect us to support them! I told them I washing my hands of them after three more years!"

"Miwa too, huh? Who da guy?"

"Hachiro Shiotsugu! I going tell his brother we the poorest family in Kahana! We six Gs in the hole. The old man all face."

"You sure about Mama? She not too old?"

"Fujie works at the hospital! Not only that, Fujie *hapai* too! My kid not even going have grandparents! My own parents competing with me! I—"

"You know, you getting more mad than you should. You—"

"What you mean, more mad than I should!?"

"Well, lots of families in Kahana like that. The guys don't crab like you."

"They zombies. They don't care if they die on the plantation! They no better than the old futts! They don't have the guts to fight back! . . ."

I leave more angry than before. *More angry than I should be!? I go nuts if I act like the gutless wonders! They all wanted to see Danny and me get beat! They called us snobs, braggarts. Both our families came to Kahana in 1935. The place was so country, every fifth family had a retarded child! . . .*

I refuse to go to Miwa's shotgun marriage.

"So, that's the kind of man I married," Fujie mumbles as she leaves.

Then Mama has a son at the hospital. Fujie sees them every day, but I refuse to go. My child is going to have an uncle only a few months older!

"Why don't you go see her?" Fujie says. "They'll be there for a week. Scott Jun is a good-looking baby."

"Why they call him Scott? We not Scotch."

"Takako picked it. She likes Randolph Scott." She laughs.

"And Jun?"

"It has the same *kanji* root as 'Kiyoshi,' Mama said. 'Jun' has a heart radical and 'Kiyoshi' a water radical. Papa picked it."

Thass one more reason for not going! Kiyo is their golden boy and now Jun is golden boy number two.

Happy's letter makes me forget my anger. My troubles are small potatoes.

A Texas division checked into camp. Immediately they ▄▄ ▄▄ ▄▄ ▄▄ ▄▄ ▄▄▄▄▄▄▄▄▄▄▄▄▄▄▄▄▄▄▄▄▄▄▄▄▄▄▄▄ But these guys were six feet and I'm only 5′4″? How was I to hit them? We had one casualty, ▄▄ ▄▄▄▄▄▄▄▄▄▄▄▄▄▄▄▄▄. Old Man Turner (both he and Capt. Lovell volunteered to come with the 100th) had warned us to turn the other cheek, but hey, we're Buddhists. Anyway Turner backed us up all the way. Takes real guts for a battalion commander to stand up to a division commander. Morale starts from the top . . .

Pals,

Happy

They censored all the part about the Texans, I write him.

Maybe you should write in pidgin. . . . We're expecting our first baby in 3 months. If it's a boy, I'll name him "Kenji" after you. . . . I'm enjoying algebra II. I always liked numbers. That's how you count MONEY. Except for the gas and liquor rationing and the mainland haole GIs on Front St. you hardly know there's a war. . . .

5

9,507 Volunteers

I sit in the cab of the truck and read the problem for the third time, but the words don't register. The blue-cellophane light bugs-out my eyes. I roll down the window and take a break.

"Hey, you jes' like 'Aburahamu Rinkon,' eh?" Shig Kodama outshouts the roar of the crushers. We all learned about Lincoln studying by the light of the fireplace in our *shushin* classes.

"You know, the only way we can get outta here is through college. For us poor buggahs, we gotta take one correspondence course and learn one trade," I yell.

"Too bad. If not for Pearl Harbor, you and Danny Lowe be fighting main event by now, eh?"

Shig is one of the few guys in Kahana who pulled for me and Danny.

"Maybe it's one blessing in disguise. You get punchy after so many fights."

"Not you. You scientific. How many fights you had?"

"About fifty. But they all three-round limit."

"I give you credit, Tosh. No give up," he says when he leaves.

The war's gonna last forever; Guadalcanal is taking forever. Then the Army announces they want 1,500 volunteers from Hawaii. They ask for 3,000 from the mainland. Together they'll form a regimental combat team to fight in Europe. The older nisei teachers like Robert Kuni and Lion Club members go around town and to the plantation camps to talk to the young guys. But lots of old guys—Masayoshi Oba, a fellow truck driver, who's 5 years older than me, Kazuma Kurio, Iwao Araki, and Toshi Ansai, the only nisei on the Maui County Board of Supervisors, volunteer.

Before the war the papers kept harping about the loyalty of the nisei. Of 400,000 people in Hawaii, Japanese were 150,000, of whom 100,000 were nisei. What if there's a war with Japan? Every admiral, general, and congressman said the nisei cannot be trusted. At the 1937 statehood hearing a nisei stood up and said as much as he hated to to see a war between America and Japan, that was the only way he could prove his loyalty, by packing a gun against Japan.

"They trying to get rid of us," Satoru Kimura from the mill says.

"How you know?"

"Too many of us."

"Naw, they giving us chance."

I think about it afterward. *Yeah, how come they asking for 3,000 from the mainland camps and only 1,500 from Hawaii? We outnumber the mainland nisei. It's because they wanna empty the camps and cut down costs.*

In a few weeks 9,507 sign up, or 1 out of 3 of guys between 18 and 38. Kiyo signs up and tells the old farts. Joji asks Papa for permission. Naturally, Papa says no. The guy will never learn. Asking the old man for permission is like handing him your balls. You act first, then tell him, "Take it or leave it." Maybe Kiyo can do that because the old farts treat him special after he got run over by the car.

Every time we turn around, there's a new name—"Swipe" Yamada from the Kahana "drunk pile," the Tsuda brothers, Nobuo 30 and Hideo 24. Do they get 1 or 2 *sembetsu?* Pepelau is quiet whereas Kahana has one farewell party after another. Guests bring *sembetsu,* or farewell money gifts. Mama sews a *sennin bari* for Kiyo.

Pepelau is a big town and lacks Kahana's sense of community. Like our neighbors, the haolefied Sakai sisters, they don't even look at you when you say "hello."

The Army changes the quota to 1,500 from the mainland and 2,900 from Hawaii. I don't blame the mainland guys. I wouldn't volunteer either if they herded me behind barbwire. The whole town goes to the courthouse to see them off. The volunteers are decked with leis over their bright aloha shirts. The plantation says it'll give them back their old jobs. Big deal.

I shake hands with all the Kahana guys—Tets Shiotsugu, Miwa's brother-in-law; Kazu Kawai, son of Ichiro Kawai, our matchmaker; Tayan Koyama . . . Camps like Kahana are placed in the middle of canefields to work the fields around them. The company houses are so open, you hear every word of the fight going on next door. You're so isolated, gossip is the only entertainment. Old Mr. Takeshita and old Mrs. Mukai are KGMB and

KGU respectively. Like it or not you get to see all the skeletons in every family's closet.

I shake hands with Nobuo Tsuda. He'd been working since 14 and sent all his siblings to high school.

"How come you going?"

"It's my escape hatch," he says with a big grin.

I'm surprised at the number of old farts. There's "Sunshine" Kashima, my classmate at Liliuokalani. We nearly got killed when we were kids. He was "packing" me on his bike on Front Street and a car hit us and ran over the bike. His father had the Japanese newspaper concession and Sunshine went to Pepelau High and straight on to Univ. of Hawaii. He made the dean's list in journalism, but the only job he could find was with the bilingual *Nippu Jiji*. My Pepelau friends are guys I grew up with from the first grade.

"Hey, Sunshine! You think you can keep up with these kids!?" I say.

"I'm in top condition, Tosh." He puts up his fists.

Fujie with her big belly drapes one lei after another on the Kahana boys. She drapes one on Sunshine.

"Too bad. I figured I'd be writing about your fighting main event at the Civic Auditorium," Sunshine says.

"So how come you going?" I ask. He has 2 younger brothers and a sister.

"I figure they need some college grads."

There are about 80, including 12 from Kahana. I don't know most of the 18–20 year olds from Pepelau, but I know the Kahana boys' older brothers and sisters.

Suddenly it's time to go. Mrs. Saito, whose husband owns Saito Bakery on Front Street, is waving a paper at the recruiting officer and pulling her son, Tadashi, from the crowd. The haole officer looks at Tadashi and shakes his head and Tadashi bursts into tears.

"What's happening?" It turns out Tadashi is only 17 and his mother brought his birth certificate. Tadashi sits on the curb and wails.

I'm so happy Mama said her good-bye in Kahana. Mothers are everywhere. Satoru Shoda is an only child of a small grocery store on Front Street. His mother holds him and cries and cries and won't let go. Poor guy is so embarrassed.

I shake Kiyo's hand last. They're already boarding the Army trucks.

"Take care, eh?" I don't know what to say. "Circle right, keep moving."

I worry, watching him climb on the truck. *The guy one loner, one bookworm. Thass why, maybe, his counters always split-second slow. He thinks too much.*

The Army trucks move slowly around the courthouse and onto Front Street. Some mothers and fathers run along the trucks. There's a stop sign at Front Street, but Kanemitsu, Kaumeheiwa, and another policeman stop the eastbound traffic and let the trucks turn right one after the other like in a funeral procession. The kids wave and wave. I get a lump in my throat and I kinda swell with pride. I think of the mainland volunteers. *How it must feel leaving the barbwire enclosures, seeing their families behind them, waving.*

6

Kiyo

I feel like I turned a corner when I finish algebra II. I can do it by myself. I'm past Fujie and her bosom buddy, Margaret. You have to take it one lesson at a time; skip one and you're lost on the next.

It's Wednesday or Thursday. I get up at 2 and fix some coffee before hitting the books. I go out to the mailbox on Back Street. It's baking hot in March. We're only a block from the ocean but the massive plantation store on Front Street blocks off the sea breeze. There's a letter from Kiyo. In it are a $6,000 cashier's check and a note:

> Won this in crap game. Pay up all the debt. I manufactured some of the luck, but I think the Oyama luck has finally turned around. Take care the body. See you after the War.

I gobble my lunch and rush to the Bank of Hawaii on Front Street and get it cashed.

Aoki Store is a block away. We owe them the most. Papa boarded Mr. Aoki long ago when he attended Pepelau High. So Papa was his *onjin*. The Bulahead say you owe your benefactor for life. Too bad. Aoki should've refused Papa credit and forced him to quit fishing. They'd arranged for me to work at the store after Liliuokalani School and on weekends to pay off the debt. I never saw a dime. When I told Rev. Kanai I was quitting language school, he said, "Wai dzu you dzu disu tsu me?" meaning, "Why do you do this to me?" His *bobura* English was so funny I cracked up. Next thing he's holding me by the collar and hitting my head with his middle knuckle. "Wai dzu you dzu disu tsu me, wai? . . ." he keeps saying and I can't stop laughing at his atrocious English.

When he stopped hitting me, he had me stand in the corner like I was in kindergarten. As soon as he turned around, I climbed out of the window and ran. It was my first day at work. I had to be at Aoki Store at 2. That night Papa wanted me to go with him to apologize. "Apologize!?" I said. "You Japanese are upside down! *He* should apologize to *me!* He hit me!" I'm quitting Sunday school, too, I told them. When I was in short pants, I thought God had a square black moustache like Rev. Kanai. When "Aburahamu" offered to sacrifice his son "Yakobu" to prove his obedience, God said, patting the air, "Dasu orai, dasu orai," meaning, "That's all right, that's all right." That was the only time God flashed a glinty smile. Several years later I was calling him *"Bigoté"* like everybody else.

One of my jobs at Aoki Store was packing two sets of white rice in brown bags. The bags for the Japanese weighed 5 pounds or 10 pounds. The bags for Filipinos at the same price weighed only 4 7/8 and 9 3/4 pounds. Then every Tuesday I bicycled to Pump Camp to take orders. "Don't take any more orders from Mrs. Yanagi. They owe us too much," Mr. Aoki kept saying. But I couldn't avoid her. She waited for me each time at the entrance to the camp. Pump Camp was the poorest of the plantation camps. It was all dust and big rocks and no trees. I worked 8 hours a day on weekdays and 10 hours on Saturdays and Sundays. Then President Roosevelt and the National Recovery Act forbade Mr. Aoki from working me all those hours since I was only 14.

"Where you get all the money?" Mr. Aoki says when I pay him $2,800.

"My brother. He won it in a crap game."

Our next big creditor is the Tani Fish Market across the Bank of Hawaii. Mrs. Tani has dark bags under her shifty eyes. Her hair is pulled back in a bun. She used to weigh Papa's catch while her husband entertained Papa in the back. They knew the old man cannot refuse a free beer. Mrs. Tani gets twisted when I ask to see the books. Papa borrowed $500 to buy the boat, paid back $300, then kept borrowing for bait, fuel, and ice. Then he borrowed $100 in 1923 to send to Grandfather. I pay her the $1,300 and ask for a receipt.

I go to Omiya Camp and pay Mr. Kanagawa for back rent, then Hida Store, Tanabe Dry Goods, who else? Oh, yeah, we owe Kanda in Kahana $1,450. I pay off Dr. Hamaguchi, the dentist, and Dr. Kawamura on Back Street behind Baldwin Park. I walk from one end of town to the other. Pepelau has only Front

Street and Back Street. The land slopes up gradually after Back Street. There are vegetable farms, houses, the Catholic Church, the train tracks, and the mill. Past the mill is Mill Camp. Kiawe Camp and Pump Camp sit in the middle of canefields, which slope up to the foot of the mountains. I'm pooped rushing around in the heat.

"We free! We don't have to give the old futts money no more!" I tell Fujie when she comes home from work. We could use the $55. She's expecting in couple of months. "You should quit work already."

I walk on air when I go to the mill. I cannot wait for my truck to fill up. I drive extra fast to dump the load of bagasse and speed up to Kahana and pay off Mr. Kanda and get a receipt. I stop by the house. Papa, Mama, Takako, Tsuneko, and baby Jun are at supper. I give Mama all the receipts.

"Who else do we owe? Kiyo won the money in *bakuchi*."

She shows the receipts to Papa.

"Where did he learn to gamble?" Mama says.

"He got lucky."

Mama brings out her ledger. Mr. Nakamura for $300, 3 others for $50 each. I write it down. That'll leave me $50. *That'll be my "agent's" fee, ha-ha.*

"Next time you go into debt, we're not going to help you!" I wag my finger at Papa. "One more thing, if I didn't insist on canceling our dual citizenship, you'd be interned by now."

"We're buying the Kuni Barbershop," Mama announces.

"What do you know about cutting hair?" I yell.

"Michie-san will teach us, or her helper, Emilio Rico-san."

"How much Kuni charging you!?"

"We're related so it's cheap."

"How much?"

"Five hundred dollars."

"Five hundred!? For two old barber's chairs and clippers and razors and junk! You got fooled! Any debt you get into from now on is *your* debt! Don't ask us to pay it!"

"We can always resell it."

"To whom!?"

"Emilio or some other Filipino. It's for Takako. She can't go work in the canefields."

"Why not?"

"No high school girl works in the canefields."

"First, you send her to high school so she can marry a high school boy! Now she's too good for the canefields! Canefield work has more dignity than barbering! Besides, nobody in Kahana goes to a barbershop! We cut each other's hair! The Kunis made a fool out of you! They sold you a failing business! I'm washing my hands of you! By the way, the debt is paid up so I'm not giving you any more of my or Fujie's pay!"

For once she cannot sass back.

Chiyako is my aunt who was born in Kahana. She married, had a daughter, and divorced her husband. Then back in 1938 when Yoshiko, the daughter, was 8, Chiyako married Takashi Kuni, older brother of Robert Kuni. Takashi was born in Kahana, but he didn't get along with his widowed mother, so he went to Japan. Chiyako and Takashi knew each other in Kahana.

So now we are related to the Kunis. *Damn them, they took advantage of the old farts and pretended it was a favor selling the junk for $500!*

I'm still fuming when I drive out. Then I see Joe DeMello, the blackout warden for the camp. "Hey, Joe, no forget put one towel on Manny Costa's head, eh!?" I yell.

Everybody makes fun of Manny's cue-ball head. He called himself our trainer, but all he did for me, Danny, and Happy was give us rubdowns. He didn't know beans about boxing, but it made him feel real big to act as our second.

I stop by at the Shishido boardinghouse and restaurant across from the pineapple cannery.

Joji is in the dorm taking a shower.

"Hey, Joji!" I yell at him. "Kiyo wen send me six Gs he won in a crap game. I wen pay all the debt so no go give the old futts money! You hear!?"

"They might still need some."

"It's up to you!"

I cannot figure out the guy. He uses his liquor ration to buy Papa a fifth of Scotch every month.

Back at the bagasse chute I feel so good I don't feel like studying. Trigonometry can wait. I go into the mill and yell over the roar of the giant crusher and grinder, "Hey, take it easy, you guys working too hard!"

I ask Shig Kodama to come wake me up in 30 minutes.

7

Danny Kenji

The censors blot out every other line in the first letter I get from Kiyo. "They must think you're a spy," I write him.

Hideo Tsuda sends me a short note after they reach Mississippi.

> They pulled down the shades on all the coaches. We couldn't get off the train till dark. Can you imagine? They were afraid we'd scare people. But we have to believe it's all for the good. We will not fail. You know what's our battle cry? "Go for Broke."

"That's what they say in crap games. It's from a song." I sing:

> Pau, pau, pau, pilikia
> Nui, nui, mai kai fine
> The night is young, we are young,
> Honey, let's go for broke.

I reread all their letters—Hideo, Happy, Seiji, Kiyo. They all have good penmanship. Back at Liliuokalani Mrs. Weimer couldn't get over how well we wrote. We all got "A"s in Palmer penmanship. It must've been the carryover from our calligraphy classes in language school.

In May Fujie has a boy at the plantation hospital. We name him Danny for Danny Lowe and Kenji for Happy. He's like a wrinkled, hairless puppy, so clinging and vulnerable.

"Why d'you name him after your boxing friends?" Fujie asks.

I think about it afterward sitting in my truck in the wee

hours of the morning. Danny and Happy were my 2 best friends since we moved to Kahana. There were other boxers from Kahana, but they never gave it their all like we did. Danny was a lean, handsome lightweight and Happy a 5'4" bantam with a thick neck, broad shoulders, short arms and legs, and long torso. When we went to Waipahu to fight their plantation, which was also owned by American Factors, Happy volunteered to fight Lucas Pasion. Nobody else wanted to fight the perennial territorial bantamweight champ, who stood 5'8" and had the build of a welterweight. Practically all the bantams and flyweights in the Islands were Japanese or Filipino. Competition was so tough anybody who got to be territorial champ usually ended up the national champ.

"How should I fight him?" Happy asked me.

"Keep on top of him, no give him punching room," I said.

He kept crowding Pasion and punching nonstop, but Pasion would sidestep and wing a right and floor Happy, but Happy kept bouncing up like a rubber doll.

Later that night we went to eat saimin. Happy couldn't chew the noodles.

"Go see the doctor," Danny said.

Pasion had broken his jaw and he didn't know it! Then he got real mad the next day when he watched us eat *chow fun*. His jaws were wired so he had to take in his food with a straw.

"You shoulda taken the count. I shoulda thrown in the towel," Manny Costa said.

Maybe now he'll quit, I thought. *He don't have a fighter's physique. The guys in Kahana must be snickering. Bulaheads are a strange bunch. "The nail that sticks out gets hammered," they say, so they hang back in groups and snicker at us stuck-outs when we get hammered.*

But Happy came back with the same old bounce. I loaned him my Jimmy DeForest "How to Box" pamphlets. He returned them, saying, "My best weapon is stamina." It was what I needed too when I turned pro.

I take off a week to help Fujie. I feel like I'm holding on to a powder puff every time I hold Danny Kenji. He's so helpless, it's scary. He cries, suckles, pisses, and shits when awake. You wish he'd sleep all the time and grow faster. But it's fun watching him gurgle and laugh and grow bigger. Once when washing his head at the bathroom sink I have a flash of Mama's face above my tilted head. *Did it happen?*

I figured it was gonna be a small adjustment, but now my sleep is out of whack. He cries in my dream. "Shut up!" I yell.

"Can you keep him awake at night so he'll sleep daytime?" I ask.

"He sleeps six to seven hours at night. Then he has his bottle and goes to sleep again."

"What if he went to bed later?"

"We have to follow *his* schedule."

I'm second fiddle now.

"Don't pamper him. We don't want a spoiled brat on our hands," I say when I see her cuddling him too much. I feel like hitting him when he cries. Most of the time I don't know if I'm asleep or sleepwalking. But it's fun watching him. His eyes pop out at every new thing he sees.

Studying at home is impossible. I give up and play with him. I feel so bushed going to work. I keep falling asleep in the cab, the books fall off my lap.

Shig Kodama bangs the door. "Hey, Tosh, da bagasse spilling!"

Happy writes from Mississippi.

Hey, thanks for naming the tyke after a *yogore* like me.

I'm up to my ears in ████████ We've gone through basic training four times! Maneuvers twice! Hundreds and hundreds of inspections and reveilles! Lemme into battle!

It was nice seeing the 442 guys. I gave Katsuto Hirata and Kosei Nakamura hell. There are at the most seven guys of draft age in Honokawai and three of us are in the Army!

The kids are so gung ho. They were mad because the Kotonks or mainland nisei had all the cadre jobs. Bunch of them ganged up on several unsuspecting Kotonks. I'd have fought with the Kotonk if I was there. Pinau, Maka, and Sharkey jumped me at the *bon* dance at Honganji back in '33. They didn't like my looks, I guess. You remember how the Pepelau gangs used to pick on us hicks. I didn't even know them. Every time I went for one of them, another guy would hit me from the side. They beat me up. But I caught up with them one on one. I really get fried when people don't fight fair.

Besides, I get along with the Kotonks. They call us "Buddhaheads." I told this one guy, "It's 'Bulahead.' Buddha's got nothing to do with it." It comes from *bobura* or "the raised-in-Japan bumpkin." *Boburahead* became Burahead, then Bulahead. It started as a putdown, then we started calling ourselves Bulaheads too.

It was old home week, seeing the guys from West Maui. Lots of good fighters from Oahu, Chinen, Maruo, Tsukano. They should make a good boxing team.

Hey, thanks again, and make sure Danny Kenji don't turn out goofy like me.

Pals,

Happy

A month later we get an uncensored letter from Kiyo in Minnesota. He, his classmate at Liliuokalani, Masaru Kondo, and old Nobuo Tsuda, the model number-one son from Kahana, transferred to the Military Intelligence Language School outside of Minneapolis. They'll train to be interpreters for the Pacific War.

"I hope he don't get captured by the Japs," I kid Fujie, "or get shot by the GIs."

In the summer of 1938 the county engineers built a football field above Pepelau High School. They cut into the side of the mountain and created a plateau like the deck of an aircraft carrier. The story was that Paul van Curtwyk, the football coach, needed a private field in which to practice so that Maui High and Baldwin High couldn't steal his signals. It sounded ridiculous. Pepelau High has about 300 day students and 150 boarders, and the other 2 schools are just as dinky. Besides, West Maui is cut off from the rest of the island by 2 miles of *pali* road that winds in and out with the rugged shoreline. One side is sheer cliff, the other a 100-foot drop to the ocean below. It takes 2 hours to get from Wailuku to West Maui. There's a wreckage of a car on the rocks below. So why would a couple dinky high schools send anybody over the *pali* to spy on van Curtwyk's scrimmages?

But they stuck to their story and played the games from 1939 at the field on the mountain slope. Attendance dropped in half. People called it a monument to the principal's stupidity. The school needed a cafeteria.

Walking to work, I cannot help but look *mauka* and notice the field. It scars the mountain. Then it comes to me. Of course! *Why we believe everything they tell us? Bulaheads are so uncritical! It wasn't the county but the Army! It's an emergency airfield. In case of war with Japan. They scared West Maui will be cut off! There're about 5,000 people in West Maui, of which maybe 250 are haoles, 2,500 Bulaheads. They scared for the safety of the 250. With the airfield up there they could fly in troops and supplies and subdue any Bulahead uprising! Wow!*

"You're getting paranoid," Fujie says.

"I don't think so. The Army is paranoid. You know why all the airplanes got destroyed at Hickam on December 7th? The Army had them all bunched in the middle of the field. They were more scared of sabotage by Bulaheads in Hawaii."

"You can't be so suspicious."

"You hafta be. Take the 100th. They been training now for over thirteen months. They must not know what to do with them. What if they not allowed to go overseas? What if they not allowed to fight once they get there?"

I write Happy about it.

In August the *Star-Bulletin* interviews several guys in the 100th. "We're not going to let down the people back home," they say. "It's our chance to prove our loyalty." They want to see action, not be a labor battalion in the rear.

8

The 100th

Danny Kenji keeps putting on weight and outgrowing his clothes. Good thing Fujie is good at sewing. There are several articles in the *Star-Bulletin* about the 442nd training in Camp Shelby. Their morale is high and the boys talk of fighting 2 enemies—the Nazis and prejudice at home.

Happy, Seiji, and all the others from Kahana are somewhere in North Africa. Then the *Star-Bulletin* reprints a *New York Times* article: "Japanese Americans: They Battle the Axis in Italy."

I finish trig and solid geometry a month ahead of schedule. Finally I get into the meat of my $500 course. Now I go to work loaded with an 18" x 24" drawing board, T-square, triangle, pencils, and eraser. I build a clamp to mount the flashlight onto the steering wheel.

Mechanical drawing is so tedious. Dimensioning and architectural lettering take so much time. I try to cut corners by drawing the lines freehand and by scaling by eye instead of using the architect's scale each time. Once I can draw freehand, I enjoy it. It's like calligraphy in language school. I'd play till the last minute and come running in, sweating all over, and rub the ink stick on the slab and pick up the brush and bang-bang, I'd copy the proverb on the blackboard and shoot out the door. The others would practice for the whole hour before handing in theirs, but the next day I was the only one with a a *ko-jo,* or "A+." My hand was even better than Rev. Kanai's. Mrs. Hashimoto, Joji's teacher, pushed her son to beat Joji. She had Kotaro practice every night. But every time there was a contest, Joji won first prize. Finally, Kotaro told his mother, "I cannot beat him. It's in his genes."

I get up groggy one afternoon and feel so happy the brat's gone. Fujie made me coffee. I pour me a cup and go out for the mail and *Star-Bulletin.* Its lead article says Joe Takata, baseball star, was killed in action in Italy.

Several weeks later I'm having coffee in the kitchen when

Fujie rushes in with Danny Kenji. "Matsuei Ajitomi and Martin Naganuma got killed!"

"Oh, yeah!? How you know?"

"Everybody's talking about it."

I get into my clothes and run out to Front Street. The sun and sparkling sea blind me. *So strange. What I expect? I thought it'd be like after a fire or earthquake, people milling.*

"Hey, Tosh, you wen hear about Matsuei and Martin?" Philip, the deliveryman for Aoki Store, stops his pickup.

"Yeah."

It takes about 3 weeks for the next of kin to be notified. Then another week to make the papers. But everybody's on the lookout for the *maké*-man jeep. Where's it stopping? Then the news spreads like wildfire. Hitoshi Taguchi, a crane operator, and Takeo Fujiyama, a surveyor, get it next—both plantation boys. Albert Neizman, a Pepelau fisherman, gets killed in the Gilbert Islands, 165th Infantry Regiment. He was drafted only 5 months ago. He'd have been deferred as an essential worker if he'd worked for the plantation.

"Did you know Haruyoshi Tateyama? Paia boy, I think. He was a boarder at Pepelau High. Class of '38. He got killed in Italy," Fujie says, looking up from the paper.

Several days later she mentions a Wallace Oshiro.

"Yeah, Hideo. I know the guy. We classmates at Liliuoka-lani!"

I keep a count of the KIAs—22 in October, 75 in November! Most from Honolulu and the Big Island. So far no KIAs from Kahana! The Buddhist and Methodist services are packed every Sunday. Fujie's mother attends both like the rest of the parents. Her brother, Seiji worries me. He's too quiet, like most Bulaheads. They *gaman* too much, get introverted.

Miwa has a daughter at the plantation hospital. I feel bad I never went to her shotgun wedding. *I should go see her. . . . Naw, Fujie wen do that already. But we in the same boat. The old farts call us "kuzu." We never measured up. "Don't worry, we won't depend on you!" Papa yelled at her when he found out she was pregnant, and she burst out crying.*

Miwa went to live with her in-laws after the wedding, and Mrs. Shiotsugu yelled at her all day, "You call this sweeping! Do it again!" flinging slippers into the yard. Miwa's husband, Hachiro, was the youngest of 7 boys and he'd been groomed for college. So his mother blamed Miwa and her big belly. Miwa would cry and walk home on the back road along the pigpens. "What are you doing here?" Mama would say and send her back. Miwa cooked and cleaned for Hachiro's parents and 5 unmarried brothers. Often when it was her turn to eat, there was no rice left. Mr. Shiotsugu, who was 20 years older than his wife, would save his share for Miwa.

"Why donchu go see her?" Fujie says. "Maxine's a real cute baby."

I shrug. I'm thankful Fujie don't bring it up again. Her younger sister, Mariko, left for Honolulu soon after graduating from Pepelau High. When she got married 6 months later, her mother and brothers were so mad they never went to her wedding. She was supposed to pay them back. Nothing is gratis with Bulaheads.

9

Happy

Now every time I close my eyes I see lines—layouts, dimension lines, lettering lines, light lines, punched-up lines. I get bug-eyed. But every time I feel like quitting, I think of the boys. There are no KIAs from West Maui in January but many from Honolulu and the Big Island. Everybody's on the lookout for the messenger jeep. The *Honolulu Star-Bulletin, Hawaii Times,* and *Hochi* keep printing articles about the 100th, including letters from the boys. They get good publicity even in the national press. They land in Salerno, and get written up when they're only 1,300 among 190,000 Allied troops there. Now the February issue of *Life* has a full-page photo of Turtle Omiya sitting cross-legged in a hospital robe, cotton swabs over his eyes. It says, "Blind Nisei American hero loses his sight at the crossing of the Volturno." Faraway names like Kwajalein, Eniwetok, Myitkyina pop up from the Pacific War. In March and April there are only a few KIA notices in the paper, none from West Maui.

Then I get another V-mail letter from Pfc. Kenji Sumida from somewhere in Italy:

Dear Fujie, Tosh, and Kenji,

Kazu, Jesse, Tsunehiro, Masayuki, Kaba, Senko, and even Toru who's a medic—got hit. But no million-dollar wounds. They'll be patched up and sent back. Damn, I wish Pasion had busted my eardrum instead of my jaw!

I still can't believe it happened. They hit us point-blank with their big guns. Blast upon blast zapping the air, wind roaring, smoke billowing, mud splattering, and screams. I can still see the guys dropping in slow motion while the thunder slithered off and came back exploding right over our heads. ███████████████████████████████████ ████████████████

Then I was hugging the mud with all my might. ██████

37

███████████████████████████████████████ One twitch
and I was dead. Was I the only one? The guy stopped crying
"Okaasan!" My ears were so stuffed I wouldn't be able to
hear him anyway. One even gets used to ear-shattering explo-
sions, the geysers of mud, and whirlwind. ████████████████
███
████

I don't know how long I lay in my cocoon of mud. Pretend
rigor mortis, I told my aching muscles and joints. I pissed in
my pants couple of times. The momentary warmth turned
freezing cold. And I remembered spearing fish below Honokawai. I'd get so involved I wouldn't come out till my lips
turned purple and my body shook.

I felt heady when dusk fell. I made it through this valley of
Death. Then it was pitch dark and I slogged ████████████
████ yards to the dike, thinking I was the only one. There were
███
███
████

It's these moments away from the lines when what happened seems unreal. Did it really happen? But you remember
them moment by moment, █████████████████████████████████
███████████████████████████. It's only when you get in
the rear, you have the luxury of thinking: who was the asshole who sent us against heavy artillery armed only with
rifles!?

████████████████████████████e order of battle. It's
taken for granted that nothing will go according to plan. But
███
███
███
███
███
██████████████████y.

So our order was to slog through 200 yards of knee-deep
mud, scale a 10-ft. dike, cross the rapid-moving river beyond
it and charge up the sharply rising ground and capture the
town along the river. Jerry had blown up every tree and building in the 200 yards, and planted mines our detectors couldn't

detect. ████████ had made it to the wall two nights ago. Now it's our turn in broad daylight under a smoke screen. Instead of a bazooka I carried a ladder. You just knew the smoke screen was going to lift. ████████████████████████████ ██ ████████████e.

Next we were ordered to take a low hill, which controls the paved road to the top of the 1500-ft. ridge. It was another trap. Jerry way up there could hit even the backside of our hill. Some low rock outcroppings were our only cover. Jim ████ got hit. We couldn't move. If you squatted to shit, their sharpshooter picked you off. Those who couldn't hold out till night shit in their pants. I was real popular, but I'd rather let go of my sphincter voluntarily than be forced to do so. We held out for four days and nights, in snow and rain, till ordered back. ██ ██████████████████████████████████████rts.

I had a fit when we got to the rear. Kosei Nakamura greeted me like I'd just come home *pau hana!* He worked as milker at the plantation dairy in Honokawai. "You crazy bastard! How come you're a rifleman!? That's the most dangerous job! Why didn't you try for Headquarters, Supply, Cook, Artillery, anything but infantry!?" I said. Even Heavy Weapons is better unless you're a forward observer. You're either on the line or in the rear. And the kid's barely five feet, hardly 100 pounds, and bright. "I volunteered," he said. I guess not so bright. It's depressing.

Well, enough bitching. We bitch and bitch but it's all *butsu-butsu.* Why can't we spew it out? Well, it won't help in the Army anyway. There's one small consolation, there's no chicken shit in the field. It used to drive me crazy in training. Sure enough, the loud-mouth officers in training were the first to crack under fire. ████████████████████████████ ██ Of course, many other haole officers, they're willing to die for us. But as I said, I'm glad I'm a private. I'm not supposed to think. Just do as they say and go on to the next job. But it's hard not to think when you're in the rear.

So how is my namesake? I give you credit plugging away at

your correspondence course. You taught yourself how to box from books so why shouldn't you learn drafting the same way?

Pals,

Call me "Lucky"

Fujie reads Happy's letter and says, "Danny Kenji needs a companion. It doesn't cost any more to raise two."

"That's right, yeah?" I reply, surprising myself. "You wanna start now?"

So many wahines getting hapai, *including a couple by their mainland G.I. boyfriends.* Fujie calls them "chauvinists." "They're ashamed of being Japanese," she said. "They want to prove they're one hundred ten percent American." "Nah," I said, "they never had a haole look at them before. Now they floored by all the *ho'omalimali.* Haoles good with the mouth. At least we mean what we say, eh?" Mama keeps her fingers crossed that no GI shows up in Kahana.

Trying for the second child adds excitement to our love-making. She don't have to act shy about spreading her legs. We go for broke. But she gets *hapai* so fast I have to go back to *ho'omali-mali* and all that foreplay.

10

100/442

No KIAs in the 100/442 from West Maui in March and April. Then in May Lincoln Kaumeheiwa's parents get the notice. Everybody knows Lincoln. He was a big fullback at Pepelau High, class of '39. He joined the merchant marine and his ship is sunk in Alaskan waters. Then Kosei Nakamura, the Honokawai boy Happy talked about, is killed in early June and gets the Bronze Star. He's the first KIA among the 442nd volunteers from West Maui. Several weeks later the papers list 2 Wailuku boys killed on the same day, June 2, 1944, near Lanuvio, Italy.

On June 5th Rome falls. The next day the Allies land in Normandy. The 100th meets up with the 442nd and becomes its first battalion but retains its "100th" name. They were called the 100th because they didn't belong anywhere. Now they have their own artillery, engineers, anti-tank, and headquarters.

Right away somebody sees the messenger jeep and the news spreads like a runaway cane fire. Masa Oba's parents get the first notice. Poor guy, he was 5 years older than me. *He wen volunteer to be one rifleman too? They should put the old farts in headquarters where it's safe, but then an artillery barrage can get you anywhere.* He drove a truck too and we used to chew the fat. Then Giichi Chinen and Sunichi Oba, no relation to Masa, are killed. I knew them enough to say "hi." We all worked for Frontier Mill. Some familiar names crop up in the newspaper's casualty list: Shigeo Wasano, Kihachiro Hotta, and Tadayoshi Iriguchi, all recent graduates of Pepelau High; and Masaru Tengan, who volunteered while still a student at Pepelau High. They were out-of-towners, boarders. Then Lt. Warren Prescott, assistant manager of the plantation store on Front Street, is killed. He was with an anti-tank group in France and is awarded the Silver and Bronze Stars.

"He was the comanager with Alan Freeland of our boxing team!" I tell Fujie.

When we took the steamship to Kauai to fight the plantation there, Happy, who just had the wires removed from his jaw, went "Cabin" with Warren, Alan, and Mr. Tyler. At supper the managers got steak while Happy got pork chops like the rest of us. Happy piped up, "We're the fighters, we put our jaws on the line. You fellas are the hangers-on. So how come you eat steak and we're relegated to pork chops? It should be the other way around." Coming back, we all had steak. Warren, like Alan, was a real nice haole.

The 100th receives a Presidential Unit Citation for its action near Belvedere in Italy. Different cities keep popping up in the papers: Livorno, Firenze, Pisa, Arno . . .

Before the war, I could count on one hand the guys who died young. Bunch of us used to climb the telephone poles to watch the pro fights at the stadium across the mill. All the fighters were Filipino or Japanese. Choei Ige from Kiawe Camp climbed a pole and grabbed a live wire and got electrocuted. Seizen Kudaka and Shozo Nishimura were stars in the plantation-sponsored barefoot football, basketball, soccer, and baseball games. They played so hard they came down with T.B. and died right away. Buster Ferrera was still a barefoot boy when he stepped on a nail and died from lockjaw.

The *Maui News* writes about Pfc. Kaoru Moto of Puunene. He's awarded a Distinguished Service Cross for destroying 3 machine-gun nests single-handedly.

"I know the guy!" I tell Fujie. "I fought him back in '37. Was my third or fourth fight. I wen beat him every round."

"Was he killed?" Fujie asks. Her *hapai* already shows.

"No, he got hit in the leg."

"That's good. Many of the DSCs are given posthumously."

"I wen talk to him after the fight. Yeah, real quiet type."

"The quiet ones are often the bravest," she says.

"You saying us talkers not brave?"

"No, but the *shibai*s tend to talk more than act."

"I not one *shibai*! I can back up my words!"

"All I'm saying is the quiet ones tend to be strong. '*Bushi ni wa nigon nashi*,' Takemoto *sensei* used to say. You talk with action, not words."

"Nah, Moto, he brave because he one boxer. Boxers gutsy."

"Moto *is* brave because he *is a* boxer," she says. "A boxer, not *one* boxer."

"Yah, yah, I know."

42

"You have to speak correctly if you want to be an architectural draftsman."

"But I can *write* good English."

"That's not enough. You have to be able to speak it."

"I feel funny acting haolefied when no haoles around."

Kiyo must be in the Pacific by now. The interpreters are supposed to be super secret, but we learn Hoichi Kubo, a Kahana boy, got the DSC for saving lots of civilians from committing suicide on Saipan. He was drafted before the war and was with the 100th in Wisconsin. Then he was transferred to the Military Intelligence Language School in Minnesota. The guy was a *bobura* type, real good in Japanese, but he was pretty good in English too.

We get a rare short letter from Fujie's brother, Pfc. Seiji of Company C. He's in a hospital in Italy. "It's not serious. Shrapnel hit my thigh. So far everybody from Kahana got hit. Even Toru, who's a medic. The medics go right out in the line of fire."

I always wake up groggy sleeping 8 A.M. till noon. Then Fujie tells me Froggy Yasui is home on furlough, and I'm wide awake. He got hit on the knee and walks with a cane. I gobble down my lunch and buy a Primo 6-pack. Hard liquor is rationed, but nobody drinks whiskey in this heat. I go to Mill Camp above the mill and ask people where his house is.

Me and Froggy go back to the first grade. The teachers always picked on us, especially Mrs. Colon, a skinny, nervous *hapa* wahine. We had a 1-hour sleeping period after lunch. When it wasn't raining we'd sleep under the *ohai* tree on our straw mats. As soon as Mrs. Colon went to the other *ohai* tree to talk story, we'd crawl to each other's mat and whisper. One day we didn't see Mrs. Colon coming back. Before we knew it she was right on top of us, whacking Froggy. Froggy wriggled like a worm back to his mat while Mrs. Colon kept whacking and whacking him. I couldn't stop laughing even after she came back and started whacking me. She stopped only after her yardstick broke.

Froggy went to work in the canefields after graduation and I went on to high school, and we lost touch until I started fighting. He came to all my fights and, win or lose, waited outside the dressing room.

His house is like any woodframe plantation house. "Plantation road" is dirt so the houses are dust covered, though not like Kahana's red dust.

"*Konnichi wa!*" I shout.

His mother comes out, dressed in a cotton print dress.

"*Oyama no Toshio desu. Ichinen sei no toki kara Haruto san no dokyu sei datta.*"

"Ah, *dozo, o-agarinasai.*"

I hand her the beer and step out of my slippers. From the veranda, the screen door opens up into the parlor, where 2 old ladies sit on wooden chairs facing Froggy on a faded couch.

"Hey, you old rascal!" the foghorn voice says.

"No get up."

The ladies get up to leave. "*Ojama shimashita....*" They begin the elaborate formalities of saying good-bye. *The Japanese waste so much time.*

Froggy hobbles on his cane to the veranda to see them off.

"You back for good? They not going send you back?" I ask as soon as he sits down.

"Not to the line anyway." He taps his right knee. "This what they call one million-dollar wound."

Mill Camp is only 5 blocks from the ocean, but the mill is like a mountain, shutting off the sea breeze. Mrs. Yasui brings out some *pupu*s.

"*Arigatai ne, Haruto-san ga buji ni kaette? Sho-gakko no toki, me-ra wa ichiban kolohe datta.*"

"Ah, *Arigataku gozaimasu.*" She bows. "*Itsumo itsumo kansha shite imasu. Oshaka-sama no okage de. Mata Okami sama no okage de ...*"

It embarrasses Froggy. He says, "Hey, come fat, eh? I bet you no can make lightweight now?"

"Naw, I can make hundred twelve easy if I quit beer. But how come you still a private? Even Happy Sumida a pfc. now. I figure you a lieutenant by now."

"Lemme tell you something. Private the safest place. I tell anybody who outranks me, 'You first, I follow.' Hey, you wen hear Poté Otake got one battlefield commission? They letting us lead platoons now. Up till now all officers haoles."

"The guy was a leader even in football. The other teams scared to run on his side of the line. He got the size too," I say.

"When you on the line, you lucky you short."

44

"So what was it like?"

He shakes his head and says nothing for a while. "A regular human butcher shop. Blood-blood-blood, bloody legs, arms, heads oozing brains, guts spilling, blood, dirt, and shit. Minute ago that was your buddy!" A tear runs down his cheek and he looks away.

Sorry.

"We had thirteen hundred when we wen land in Salerno. Before Cassino we already down to eight hundred. We lose three hundred more at Cassino. Companies E and F was extra rifle companies. They got used up in no time. Everybody got hit—Jesse, Poté, Mike, Jimmy, Senko . . . everybody."

"Except Happy."

He laughs. "Yeah we call him 'Ghost.' What a goofball. That's the way to last, maybe. But three of his ammo carriers got killed. Now nobody wants to carry his ammo. So he volunteer to carry the ammo if the other guy carry the bazooka. The guy look like one bazooka too."

"You think they using you guys for cannon fodder?"

"Yeah, we all bitched about it, but the other two battalions wen get clobbered too. Haole kids from Minnesota, Wisconsin, around there. Before that two regiments from Texas got wiped out trying to cross the river. We all had the same order: cross the Rapido and take the town of Cassino. Those guys scaled the dike at least. We'd be wiped out if we got over. We'd leave the ladders behind and be too short to climb back. Nobody would've made it back."

"D'you know Kaoru Moto? Puunene boy. I fought him back in '37. Decision. He won a DSC. He KO'd three machine-gun nests by himself."

"Yeah, he was in Charlie company. I wen read about it. That was after Cassino. You know, war one contest in *gaman.* Who can take more shit. When the *gaman* snap, you no give a shit no more, and you stand up and go banzai-charge a machine-gun nest."

"How long you staying?" I say when I get up to leave.

"Tomorrow."

"I thought you had a week furlough."

"Yeah, but I gotta go."

"Why?"

"I feel bad. All the guys who *maké.* I come back and they

look at me like I one hero. The mothers, they come see me. It's like they asking me, how come their sons *maké* and I alive? I don't know what to say."

He hobbles out to the veranda.

"Hey, no worry, they going give you back your job."

"Hey, I get only one good leg! No go pull it, eh!?"

"Tomorrow we go Liliuokalani and see Mrs. Colon."

He busts out laughing. "You *kolohe* boy! You was bad influence!"

I feel good when I can leave um laughing.

11

The Lost Battalion

September is quiet. Then suddenly the messenger jeep is spotted everywhere. People run after it to see where it will stop. Yoshio Tengan is killed in France, then Tokio Ajitomi, whose older brother was killed last October in Italy. Then two more of Fujie's classmates get it: Hideo Shigeta and Lt. Poté Otake. Poté gets the SS and DSC. There are new French names—Bruyeres, Biffontaine, Vosges. *What's happening? What's happening? Are they on the main front?* The papers write them up: "They're small and quick, they take cover expertly, advance without disclosing their positions, and don't retreat."

They lift martial law. Front Street lights up like a Christmas tree. Now I can throw away the flashlight and study in a fully lit cab. I pass the exams in sections and details, and go on to specifications. Fujie is big with our "love" child.

Harry Bridges, Jack Hall, Louis Goldblatt, Thompson, Yagi, many others go into the canefields to talk to the workers on their breakfast and lunch breaks even though field-workers are not eligible to join a union. Louis Goldblatt is a hero to Bulaheads. He blasted the internment of the West Coast Japanese as "a dark page of American history" when nobody else said anything.

Most of the field-workers, except for the mostly Japanese *hanawai* men, are Filipinos. Nisei make up most of the mill workers and tractor operators. Portuguese handle the giant grabbers. Except for the *luna*s and some of the machine operators, everybody's for the union. I join right away along with the mill workers. "The tougher the boss, the easier the job," Jack Hall says, and Jack Carlyle is the biggest SOB in Hawaii. He was born and raised in Hawaii, but he acts like a mainland haole. He kicked out the whole Hamaguchi family from Kahana when Mr. Hamaguchi got pulled in by the FBI after Pearl Harbor.

The 1,067 workers at Frontier Mill are 60 percent Filipino and 40 percent Japanese. The Filipinos went on strike in 1937 and the Japanese in 1920, and each time the other race broke up the strike. Now the union preaches "brotherhood."

The Sixth Army lands in Leyte and the Russians capture Belgrade. The Japanese navy is smashed in the battle of Leyte Gulf. The 100/442 rescue the Lost Battalion. *How did they get lost? They had no compass?* Just when I think the war is winding down there are more KIAs in the paper. Now they're 18 and 19 year olds. Mitsuichi Yoshigai, a 442nd volunteer, gets an SS. He's the second carpenter from Frontier Mill to die.

The papers say the 100/442 liberated Bruyeres and Biffontaine and rescued the Lost Battalion. I keep a count—49 killed in October. Many Kotonks. *How the parents must feel, living in barracks behind barbwire, getting the telegram, "We regret to inform you . . ."*

The *Honolulu Star-Bulletin* starts printing dispatches from a Lyn Crost, a war correspondent in France and Italy. She interviews Hawaii GIs in the 100/442 and generals who praise the "Buddha-heads." Joseph Farrington and his paper were always friendly to the nisei. It's the icing on the cake, except now me and Happy are the only "Bulaheads."

Kahana has 10 in the 100th and 14 in the 442nd, but so far not one KIA. Honokawai, Happy's hometown, has only about 6 Japanese families, who work the plantation dairy and the pump station. They have 3 in the 100/442, and 1 KIA.

There are big write-ups about the rescue of the Lost Battalion. The newsreel at the Frontier Theatre shows the guys linking up with the happy Texans. Later I learn they had over 800 casualties to rescue 211. The 100/442 is awarded more Presidential Unit Citations. *Enuff already. They wen prove their loyalty several times over.*

November 7, 1944 is our first election in 4 years. ILWU reps come by and ask us to vote for its slate of candidates. Before the war the Democrats were a joke. In the '38 election I was Minoru Shiotsugu's helper and too young to vote. We rounded up the eligible voters from the canefields. Joe O'Connor, the harvesting field boss, rode with us. He mumbled to each guy, "You know how to vote," and led his yes-men into the courthouse while I waited in the truck.

"You wen vote Democratic?" I asked Minoru later. "What you take me for? The pencil tied to one string. Joe stay right behind you. I get fired on the spot," he said. "How come nobody gutsy enough to give it a test run? You can always say, 'Was one mistake!' I said." But a week later I got proof. Mrs. Walker, a newcomer from Utah, taught social studies at Pepelau High. She voted for David Trask for delegate to Congress. That night Jack Carlyle stormed to her cottage up on the high school campus and demanded to know why she'd voted for Trask. (It was supposed to be a close election, but Samuel Wilder King won by nearly 2 to 1.) She told Carlyle it was none of his business how she voted; besides, how did he find out how she voted—it was against the law! She mentioned it to Fujie and another of her "A" students. (That was when I started taking a second look at Fujie.) I voted for the first time in 1940, and sure enough the pencil was tied to a lever overhead, and I voted Republican down the line.

The '44 election is a shocker! Democrats capture 15 of 19 House seats and 6 of 8 Senate seats! Fourteen of the 15 were endorsed by the Political Action Committee of the ILWU! They did it all in less than a month of organizing!

Happy has not written since he shit in his pants. "Go write in pidgin," I wrote him. *No news is good news.* We don't hear from Kiyo or Seiji, either.

Then we get a letter from S/Sgt. Kenji Sumida.

Dear Fujie, Tosh, and Kenji,

I stay hospital. Dry clothes, warm, hot food, real bed, but no can *moemoe*, too much *huhu*. Every time *hanapaa* 目 see *taisho* ダルクイス *ichiban kuso*. He *rikugun taisho* only 三月. Before office job. Know nothing infantry. But he want make name. So he push-push. "How long you wen stay in dis foxhole? Get out and charge!"—just li'dat. He *holoholo* da front, look for men, give *manini* orders. He wen see Poté and his platoon in reserve when looking for rest of us. He order Poté to attack! You no can attack onry one platoon. Suicide. He wen *maké* Poté! He almost wen *maké* us. We take one hill. Take another one by 1200, he says. We take by 1500. Come right down, he says. What about leaving some men? We say.

49

No! Turns out that hill belong to another div. They retook it with heavy losses. That's the kind of *kuso* ダルクイス is.

He wen lose da battalion. He wanna show up the other *taisho*s so he push-push, no consolidate. We almost wen get lost too. We take one town. He push. Take another one more far away. No sense. No military value. Jerry cut us off if stay longer. Real *kuso!* He call middle firefight. Ask why not advancing? One time Kim yanked the phone dead. Back in training I call the *Yobo* chicken-shit ninety-day wonder but he more samurai than us. Captain Kim wen save me twice.

So *kuso taisho* push this battalion till they get cut off on top mountain. They belong first regiment who get beat back. Why no call second regiment? No, he tell *us:* Rescue all cost! He desperate. *Okole* on line. But he get us by *okintama*. No can play army game like one and two regs. We all *Nihonjin*. *Hyoban* on the line, alla time, alla time.

But lucky again. Two days before get hit. Walk to rear, ride to hospital. Poor guys, all tired, eight days fighting, now go into thick forest, dripping fog, freezing. I think I *maké*. Piles of WIAs come in. Lots of new-type treeburst wounds. Ugly. Couple from my squad. I made leader because nobody left but me and Kotonk kids they wen draft from the camps. "No send me replacements on the line!" I wen yell and yell. They barely 18 with four months training. They terrified. They corpses before I get to know their names.

So save Texas lost battalion. 140 of us *maké*, 710 wounded to save 210. Get general's ass out of sling. He push-push-push just for promotion.

Hope the noncombatant shavetail no wen censor me this time.

Give my namesake a hug. Flattered to be so remembered.

Pals,

Happy

"*Da-ru-ku-i-su* must be something like Dalquis, eh?" I say, handing the letter to Fujie. "What kind name, that?"

I answer him right away. They didn't blot out a word of his letter.

"He should get a girlfriend and get married when he gets out," Fujie says.

"Same thing with your brother," I say. *So many guys end up bachelors. Not only that, they don't even date.*

12

VE Day

In December Marcia Hisaye is born at the plantation hospital. I take a week off from work to look after Danny Kenji. What a luxury to sleep through the night!

But Marcia's left foot is turned inward.

"It's a clubfoot," Dr. Hall says.

"What can you do for it?"

"Nothing. Massage it."

"Will that straighten it?"

"Sometimes."

"Will she be able to walk?"

"She might limp a little, but massage will help. And practicing to walk straight early on."

Gimme a break! But now every time I pick her up I instinctively massage her foot.

There's a lull in the news and casualties. The Army says the interned Japanese can return to the West Coast in January. In late November B-29s raid Tokyo from the Marianas. Just when I think it's winding down the Germans launch a big offensive in the Ardennes. Bastogne holds out, then the weather clears on Christmas day and the Allied planes catch the Germans in the open fields without air cover.

Masa Ida from Kahana is back. He's shell-shocked. He sits on the swing in their backyard and runs into his parents' house every time anybody comes near.

Things happen so fast. The Sixth Army lands on Luzon, MacArthur returns to the Philippines, the marines land on Iwo Jima. Then the last Japanese position in Manila is wiped out. Iwo Jima falls after 36 days. Over 25,000 American casualties, nearly 7,000 marines killed and 21,000 Japanese.

I worry about Kiyo. *Where is he? I don't think he go in the first wave. But how can he interrogate prisoners if they don't surrender?*

On April 1 the Army lands on Okinawa and the Japanese counterattack with kamikazes. The Okinawan families left in Kahana, including Fujie's mother, whisper and worry about their relatives. It's only 65 miles long and 6–8 miles wide, so they're bound to get caught in the cross fire.

Soon after they lifted martial law many Okinawan families left Kahana for Honolulu. I don't blame them. The *naichi* Japanese treated them as second class. When I was running around in short pants, we used to call Okinawans "Big Rope." *Ookii nawa* means "big rope." Fujie says she used to cry when they called her that. I thought it was harmless. Okinawans are good boxers. Many KIAs in the 100/442 have Okinawan names.

The 100/442 go into action again in Italy. *I hope General Dalquis is gone.*

Ever since Mama bought the barbershop and learned how to cut hair, I stop by between dumping bagasse when I need a haircut. Papa built a private bathhouse in the back so now Miwa can have a few minutes of peace when she brings baby Maxine to bathe. Business is bad at the barbershop. The only clients are the Filipino bachelors. The same ones come night after night to get shaved by Takako. Every time Mama says she'll do it or Emilio can do it, they say no, they want Takako and they wait in line. They lie in the barber chair and stare at Takako while she's shaving them. Mama dares not leave Takako by herself. The Filipinos were not allowed to bring their women to Hawaii.

"I told you! The Kunis sold you a failing business! They pretended they were doing us a favor because we're related!"

"We can sell it to Emilio and get our money back."

"Don't call on us if you go into debt again!"

At the entrance of the camp is *luna* row, the fancier houses and yards of the Portuguese, nisei, and Filipino *luna*s. Manny Costa, our "trainer," is in his front yard, trimming the hisbiscus hedge. He's completely bald.

"Hey, Manny, how come you no wear your hat?"

"Hey, champ."

"Hey, pound for pound, the 442 just like me, eh? They the best fighters in the Army."

"Yeah, just like the Japanee Imperial Army, eh?"

I kill the engine and jump down. "What you mean!?" I'm ready to hit him even if he's an old man.

"Well, they're both good fighters."

"Shit! We not like them! They fight just one way! We slip, duck, sidestep, counter, right cross! We can think on our feet! The Japs, they no can improvise, all they can do is follow orders!"

"I only kidding you." He laughs.

"Oh, yeah!?"

"You wanna make something of it?" He drops the clippers and puts up his dukes.

"Naw, just your form scare me." I wave him off and get back into the truck.

"Take care, champ, and no go be so touchy."

"Fock you, you Porogee."

He laughs. "Okay, you Bobora."

The bagasse is overflowing the chute when I get back.

Night life blossoms in Pepelau. It's a good thing I'm through with all the dimensioning and lettering. The final lesson is an introduction into design and sketch techniques—using tracing and graph papers, drawing perspectives, doing programs and renderings, which I really enjoy.

Joji now hangs around with Hiroshi Sasaki, the professional gambler who fronts as a cab driver. Hiroshi is a real handsome kid, son of the best sumo wrestler in Maui. He's got his father's good looks but not his size. He runs a gambling syndicate. His men take Las Vegas-type crap games to the plantation camps on Sundays. Joji's not part of his syndicate, but he runs a blackjack game at the cannery. His creditors come to me to ask him to pay them back; they know he has the money since he wins all the time.

"I pay them back half," Joji says. "If I pay them all back, they going lose it."

"So when you going pay them the other half?"

"I jes' holding it for them."

The guy turns everything around. Whenever I crab, he says I should be thankful Papa is not like the *paakiki* old farts or successful like old Mr. Kanda, who took his family back to Japan. He always sided with the old farts and always bought Papa whiskey with his ration card. Now he has Mama sew him zoot suit pants, big pleats with small pegs. He dangles a long key chain and signs his name "Georgie." Fujie tells me people are talking about his running after Evelyn Kikawa. Evelyn's a Pepelau girl, 3 years older than me, married to a Kahana boy, and who now lives in Pepelau. She likes to play around, people say. She always wore short shorts and wriggled her ass if you were walking behind her. Fujie never cared for her. "She acts like you're not there. She just talks to the men or asks you to give a message to them." Like what? I asked. "Like when the poker game is going to start."

Just when we think there'll be no more KIAs, Sadao Kawa-moto is killed in Italy in early April. He was drafted in August '44. He'd taken carpenter shop at Pepelau High, then worked in Honolulu. They were drafting niseis now, but he would have been deferred if he worked on the plantation.

April brings another shocker: FDR dies. You thought he was gonna live forever. Then Manuel Freitas, a fisherman from Pepelau with the 27th Infantry Division, is killed in Okinawa. The 100/442 crack the Gothic line in 2 days when other units couldn't for 2 months. They get their seventh Presidential Unit Citation. A Kotonk, Sadao Munemori, gets the Congressional Medal of Honor, the first for the 100/442. He threw himself on a grenade and saved his buddies. Haole soldiers were given the CMH for the same thing, so they had to give it to him. As Froggy said, many Kotonk and Bulahead's DSCs should've been CMHs, and the 100/442 could've been the first unit into Rome, but they got held back just outside of Rome so that another unit could get the honor.

On May 2 the war in Italy ends. Five days later Germany surrenders.

Couple weeks later my letter to Happy is returned. It's stamped: Missing in Action. I rush up to the plantation office where his older brother works. The plantation gave office jobs to the bright high school graduates.

"What happened?" I show Hiromi my returned letter. The war was over. Nobody was looking for the messenger jeep.

"They never found his body or dog tag," he says.

"Maybe he got hit and disoriented and walked away."

"Maybe."

"Better yet, maybe he went AWOL."

"No. He could've gotten garrison duty stateside after he was wounded. He chose to go back to his squad," he explains.

"Why don't we check with them?"

"They were Kotonks."

"The platoon leader should know."

"Yeah, I trying to find out."

"Ask Ben Moriyama, he should know."

"I did already. Nothing."

"Lemme know when you find out."

"Yeah."

Later I tell Fujie, "You know, I expect him to come bouncing in here any time." He had this distinctive bounce in his steps. He looked like a *Bobura* with his short porcupine hair.

13

VJ Day

The battle of Okinawa ends July 3. The Japanese commander and his staff commit suicide. Over 14,000 Americans are killed; 80,000 Japanese. And about 130,000 Okinawan civilians, one-third of the population of Okinawa. Now B-29s take off from Okinawa and firebomb the Japanese cities.

One night Satoru Kimura comes out of the mill and says, "The air raids killing the wahines and babies."

"The Japanee wen bomb Shanghai the same way."

"Yeah, but not like this, eh?"

"What about Nanking? They wen kill 200,000 Paké civilians."

"Yeah, but now we talking millions. You watch. When they invade Japan, they going put the 442nd in the first wave," he says, and goes back into the mill.

The guy is so negative! If there's anything shitty, he'll dig it out, dump it on you, and run. He knows how to shake you up.

They cannot do that. They wen prove their loyalty already. But I cannot go back to my studies for a long time.

The days are so hot I sweat in my sleep. Marcia cries and cries. I rub her foot, trying to turn it outward. Thank God, I'm near the end of my drafting course. *Where's Kiyo? He was in the Philippines. Did he go to Okinawa?*

I go back to Kahana for another haircut. Driving back, I see Takemoto *sensei* going to the community bathhouse. He's in his denim work clothes and carries the small bath bucket, towel, and *yukata*. He looks tan and skinny.

"Hello, *sensei!*" I haven't seen him since our wedding.

"Oh, Toshio-san." He nods.

I kill the engine. "What do you think, the Japanese will fight to the last man? Why can't they quit when they're getting beat so badly? In boxing we throw in the towel. Why can't they surrender? Why do they feel so much shame?"

"You know, the samurai never felt disgraced by surrendering. In fact, Minamoto no Yoritomo always tried to persuade his enemies to surrender. Even during the Russo-Japanese War the few soldiers who surrendered weren't ostracized. It's only in recent years. In the Shanghai incident a Japanese officer was taken prisoner when he was unconscious. When the Chinese repatriated him, he felt so ashamed he went to where he was captured and committed suicide. It made the headlines in Japan, and the military made it their code of behavior."

"*Ah so!* When was this?"

"Hmmm, 1932 or 33."

"But they all believe it now?"

"It's frightening how easily people are misled."

"So what do you think? The Japanese race will be *pau?*"

"Hmmm." He rubbed his fingers against his thumb. "I hope not."

"Me too."

I start the engine. I remember my bagasse.

"Well, take care, *sensei.*" I shift into low.

I tell Fujie later, "The guy's so smart, how come he gets stuck in a shithole like Kahana?"

Then Fujie tells me when I get up past noon. A new type of bomb destroyed Hiroshima.

"Listen," she stands next to the radio, bouncing and shushing Marcia.

We tick off the names of Kahana families from Hiroshima —Miyake, Ishida, Sakamoto, Tanoue . . .

Russia declares war, Nagasaki is bombed, and Japan surrenders. Cars go honking around town, but it's mostly the haoles and Portuguese. They own most of the cars.

"Hey, they coming home, eh?" guys say, faces lighting up. The old folks look relieved too. Now they can find out if their relatives are still alive in Okinawa, Hiroshima, Nagasaki, Tokyo, and the other cities.

The real celebration starts when the vets start coming home. Seiji is one of the first. Mrs. Nakama hires the Tsuda car and goes to the Kahului airport to welcome him. A steady stream of cars goes to Kahului to welcome home the heroes as they straggle in. *How must it feel for a Kotonk to go "home" to an internment camp?*

My mother-in-law throws a party big enough for a wedding. The whole camp shows up. I stop by between dumping bagasse. Seiji, like most Bulaheads, is not a talker. The guests have to draw him out with polite questions: "Where were you wounded?" "What was it like?"

He answers in monosyllables, and laughs.

After a long pause, he says, "Before Bruyeres, my buddy, Hachi Kiyonaga from the Big Island, he wen give me his watch. 'I not going make it,' he said. 'Caw-mon, no be silly,' I wen tell him. 'No, for real,' he said. 'Okay, I'll give it back tomorrow,' I said. He got hit by a sniper. Went right through his helmet. How he know?" He shakes his head and falls silent.

Mrs. Nakama's letters to her uncles in Okinawa are returned.

Papa gets a letter from his father in Tokyo. They had all survived—Takao, Haru, Chiyako, and her daughter, Yoshiko. Can he send some foodstuff? In Mama's family, her sister's third son was killed in the Philippines, the first and second sons have returned home, but the second is sick with T.B. There are no medicines in Japan, her sister writes. Could Papa send them some streptomycin?

Seiji goes back to his old *hanawai* job irrigating the fields.

"That's the lowest job on the plantation. You got the GI Bill. Why don't you go to school?" I say.

"I gotta look after my mother," he says.

"You wen do enough already. Let your brothers look after her."

He shrugs.

"You only twenty-eight and you give up already?" The guy's been working since 14.

"Once you been through the war, everything else small potato."

"What you mean?"

"Cannot explain unless you been there."

"So give me a hint."

"Everything else slow motion."

"All I know is it give you a good excuse to cop out. You get wounded twice so you can come back to *hanawai*?"

"You no can understand."

"Go talk to your brother," I tell Fujie.

Three Kahana boys don't come home. One gets a discharge in New York to study art, another reenlists to stay in Europe. Nobuo Tsuda worked at the plantation store for 14 years and sent all his siblings to Pepelau High. Now at 32 he says he's done enough as number-one son. He reenlists to go to Japan. He's not coming home, he says, except for his funeral.

A month later Joji enlists in the Army. He tells Papa and Mama he was drafted. *Why does he hafta lie?* His affair with Evelyn is a scandal in Pepelau and Kahana, and her husband files for divorce.

"I dint cause it. They already separated when I came in," Joji says.

"Yeah, but everybody says you the cause."

"They wrong."

He plans to spend 3 years in Germany. "The whole thing will blow over by then."

"You mean you going marry her?"

"Yeah, I love her."

"She got two kids already."

"You go talk to them, eh?" Joji asks.

"You want me to talk to Papa!? Shit, we never saw eye to eye!" *You and me, we never see eye to eye either.* It fries me when he uses me as his messenger.

"It'll blow over in three years," he says.

When I talk to Papa, he says Joji's marrying her would be like his stealing a brother's wife. It'd be so shameful, the family would have to move out of West Maui.

Mama was so relieved when Yukio Tanji started courting Takako. He'd come to the barbershop every night and walk Takako home when she closed at 9. Emilio, her Filipino helper, had been walking Mama and Takako home and he resented Yukio. But Yukio was big for a Japanese, a sumo wrestler, 150 lbs.

"You going with the son of the town drunk!" I told Takako.

"Yuki no drink," she said.

I used to see Yukio's father passed out in the parks. Yukio would go and take him home.

His father is tall and good-looking like Anshan, or Sadao Ono, my second cousin. Both are too young to fit in with the old farts, but too old for us. They're like the *kibei*s who were sent to Japan to study. They came back speaking atrocious English and even more atrocious pidgin, and they tried hard to be one of the boys.

There was a big crap game every payday at the single men's quarters, and the younger niseis, Masa, Sam, Koji, and others would get Tanji drunk and win all his pay. While the beer and money lasted, Tanji would be the life of the party. When he lost everything, he'd go home and beat up his wife or kids.

It was Koji Inouye's job to lure Tanji to the beer and crap game on payday. They called him "Hopalong" behind his back because he limped. Both he and Tanji worked in the Kahana machine shop, and Hopalong acted like he was Tanji's best friend. Even Hiroshi Sasaki and his gang in Pepelau were not so chintzy. Yukio had to grow up fast. He became a father to his much-younger siblings. But poor as they are, they send all their kids to high school and never dumped a 6-G debt on them. Mrs. Tanji had to work in the fields to keep the family afloat.

Every time Yukio and Takako stayed out in the yard past 10, Papa would come out to the veranda and wind his big alarm clock. He wanted to make sure Takako didn't get pregnant like Miwa. Mama sells the barbershop to Emilio, and Yukio and Takako get married by Rev. Sherman at the Kahana Methodist Church. Takako got an "A" from Mrs. Sherman's English class at Pepelau High. "You know why?" Takako said, explaining her only "A." "I'm active in the Epworth League, that's why."

I see Miwa for the first time since '44. She's big with her second child.

"How they treating you?"

"Okay."

"You getting enough to eat?"

She nods.

I cannot talk too much. Her husband and relatives are all around her.

Fujie and Yukio were classmates at Pepelau High. All the Nakamas, Tanjis, Shiotsugus, Kunis, and Oyamas are at the wedding, together with the rest of the camp. *I might run down the old farts but us Oyamas are smarter and better-looking than any of them.*

Kiyo comes home in late October. He catches a ride from Kahului and shows up at the house late in the afternoon in his khakis and staff-sergeant stripes.

"How come you never called us!? We come get you!" I scold him. All the guys get discharged at Schofield Barracks outside Honolulu and call from there.

He shrugs. "Easier this way."

He's still skinny and stoop shouldered, but now he chainsmokes and cannot stop jiggling.

I drive him to Kahana on my bagasse run.

"Why didn't you call Kahana Store?" Mama says.

The next day Mama, Takako, and Miwa work all day and put out a spread like New Years. Papa brings out the low table and sets it in the parlor. The 100th and 442nd vets glow with pride even when they don't talk much. You can feel it.

But the nisei intelligence work in the Pacific is still hush-hush. The papers write a lot about the 100/442, but not one word about the interpreters. Maybe that's why Kiyo talks like he's angry.

". . . Interrogating POWs was easy. They taught us in intelligence school how to be tough interrogators, but you didn't need any technique. Just a little kindness, like offering him a cigarette. Then all you had to do was ask him and he told you everything. He wasn't supposed to be captured so he got no instructions on how to act."

The parlor is packed. Everybody is bathed and in his Sunday best and comes with a welcome-home gift.

"He felt no connection with his former unit. When he surrendered, he was considered dead by his unit, so now he owed no allegiance to them. He was a dead man talking. He—"

"What are you talking about?" Mr. Yoei Sato, who just sat down, asks.

"*Horyo no jimmon,* Kiyo says.

"German prisoners?"

"No, Japanese prisoners."

"*Baka!*" Mr. Sato shouts. "A Japanese soldier never surrenders!"

"They surrendered," Kiyo says.

"A Japanese soldier kills himself first!" Mr. Sato jumps up. He used to be a private in the Japanese army in the 1920s.

"Japan lost the war, there were bound to be prisoners," Papa says.

"Japan did not lose! Japan won! Everything the papers and radios say is a lie! We're going to Honolulu to welcome the Imperial fleet!"

"*Bakatare!*" Papa says. "Everybody's laughing at you."

"Japan lost," Takemoto *sensei* says.

"We'll get you all when the Imperial Army lands!" He storms out into the night.

We all sort of look away.

Then Kiyo says, "We were one of the first into Manila. The Japanese marines bayoneted women and children, they bayoneted them not once but over and over. Piles and piles of rotting corpses. It wasn't an organized rampage, but it wasn't a stray happening, either. You have to see—"

"You know, the plantation bosses spreading those stories to the Filipinos. They wanna break up our union," Bill Toda says. He's a tall, skinny guy who quit boozing when he got to be the Kahana union rep. He goes on, "We talking 'solidarity' and 'brotherhood,' and they talking Manila atrocity."

Kiyo sighs. "Well, it happened. You can never forget it if you've seen it."

"Yeah, but what it got to do with us?" Bill says.

"Lots of the POWs I interrogated were kids my age. I used to wonder, 'What if my folks never came to Hawaii?' "

"Lucky come Hawaii, eh?" Minoru Shiotsugu says.

"All I know is the plantation trying to bust up our union," Bill says. "The only weapon they got left is to inflame the Filipinos against us with atrocity stories."

"They're not stories, they happened," Kiyo says.

"You only add fuel to the fire." Bill gets red in the face.

"The same thing must've happened in Nanking. But there the perpetrators were not battle-hardened marines but conscripts like you and me," Kiyo says.

"What do you think of their arresting General Yamashita?" Takemoto *sensei* asks.

"I don't know. They're trying to blame him for Manila."

"It's for revenge," Bill says. "It was a racial war. How come they never rounded up the Germans and Italians on the mainland? How come they never dropped the atomic bomb on Germany!?"

"Is it more cruel to bayonet innocent civilians than to incinerate them from the air?" Takemoto *sensei* says.

"But the Japanese were bombing innocent civilians in China in 1937. Hiroshima and Nagasaki would not have happened without Pearl Harbor," Kiyo says.

"They would never have atom-bombed Germany," Bill says.

"Maybe not. The German army surrendered when it lost twenty percent of its men," Kiyo says. "The Japanese were ordered to fight to the last man."

"Well, anyway, no go help the bosses, no go spread these stories." Bill gets up to leave. "Know your class and be loyal to it," he says as he steps out to the veranda.

New guests arrive with gifts, expecting to hear stories of heroism. But Kiyo is like a broken record. He hammers away at Takemoto *sensei*, ". . . Is it all based on bullying? Yesterday's bride becomes today's mother-in-law. You keep passing on the abuse? Where were the dissenters?"

" 'The protruding nail gets pounded.' " *Sensei* quotes an old proverb.

"It's pounded by the other nails?"

"No, it's the *kempeitai*. The Communists were the only protesters and the *kempeitai* crushed them. Then the fanatics took care of the moderate politicians," *sensei* says.

Yeah, remembering the argument I had with Papa. "Shoot over here!" pounding his chest, the one politician said to the young soldiers, according to Papa. Next day the Star-Bulletin *says the killers had to drag the slobbering politician from under the table.*

Sensei rubs his fingertips against his thumb and says, "It's given a new meaning to *gekokujo,* where the bottom defeats the top, the way the rice at the bottom of the pot gets on top in the serving bowl. The fanatics need not get on top. They get their way by intimidating the leaders with violence and threats of violence."

I remember my bagasse and leave the wake.

I stop by the next day and tell Kiyo, "No go live too much in the past."

"I gotta get away," he says.

"What you going do?" I ask.

"I going to New York. Get a high school diploma, then go to Columbia. GI Bill will give me five hundred a year for tuition and books plus seventy-five a month living expenses."

"You going be a teacher?"

"Naw."

"What you going study?"

He shrugs. "Something about Japanese history maybe. I wanna find something. I feel like I've been lied to all my life."

"You get taken in too easy. You gotta cut everything you hear in half. Like everything Papa or Joji tell you."

"Why do you have to go so far away? Why don't you wait till the new semester in January?" Mama says.

"No, I want to go now," he says, and leaves after 2 weeks with his $300 mustering-out pay.

"He scared the escape hatch might close," I tell Fujie.

Now Papa has only Tsuneko and Jun at home. He gets an easier ditchman job. It pays less than *hanawai,* but it'll be enough for the 4 of them. He rides his old mare to the different fields to open the irrigation gates in the mornings. Then he sits in his ditchman shack and waits for orders from the water *luna* and carves getas and clothes hangers from koa, which grow wild in the gulches.

In November I finish my course 6 months ahead of schedule. My final exam is the working drawings and specifications of (1) a residence and (2) a restaurant. They give me 6 weeks. I work around the clock and finish it in 4. I get an "A" and my diploma.

"Here, look at it," I tell Fujie. "Next time you see your friend, Margaret, tell her I'm way ahead of her."

I send out applications to a dozen firms on Oahu. Except for an Andrew Mori and couple other Bulaheads all the architects are haoles.

"I have to get out before they strike," I tell Fujie.

When Joe Santos, a Borinque *luna*, tries to disrupt Louis

Goldblatt's speech at the Palace Theatre on Front Street, the guys bounce him. Plantation labor is 60 percent Filipino, 40 percent Japanese. The ILWU don't want the niseis to dominate the leadership, so they ask them to step back and let the Filipinos, Hawaiians, and Portuguese fill some of the offices. For racial harmony. It's the only way they can beat the plantations.

Before the year is over, there's a series of articles in the *Star-Bulletin* and the bilingual *Hawaii Times* about the trouble the Kotonks are having returning to the West Coast from the internment camps. A Mary Masuda is threatened by the new haole neighbors when she returns to the family farm near Santa Ana. The papers pick it up and it's front-page news. Her brother, Kazuo, was killed in '44 as he covered the withdrawal of his men from the north bank of the Arno River. Now they give him a posthumous DSC at a rally in Santa Ana. Speakers include "Vinegar" Joe Stilwell and Ronald Reagan, the actor and Air Force captain. Even Walter Winchell gets into the act. It's funny how you get help from unexpected places. The liberals you expect help from piss on you. Like Earl Warren, Walter Lippmann, and FDR.

There are no more questions about our loyalty. The 100/442 had over 700, or 80 percent, of Hawaii's KIAs and 18,000, or 88 percent, of WIAs. They fought 225 days and won more decorations for valor than any other unit its size and length of service in American history.

II
1946-1957

14

The Strike

We're all gung ho about the union. Carlyle tries to bribe the local union reps, but he gets nowhere. I'm all for the guys, but I have to get out before they strike. December, January, and February don't worry me. Nobody hires during those months anyway. But I sweat in March and April. *How come nobody building when there's a big housing shortage in Honolulu?* I go back to the library to look up architects I might have missed.

In May the house turns into a pressure cooker. I cannot sleep. I get up and massage little Marcia's foot. When Danny Kenji was her age, Fujie kept telling me, "You're being too hard on him." But Danny Kenji cried so much and disturbed my study and sleep. Now I'm used to being groggy and sticky all the time and I'm finished studying at home. Besides, Marcia is a little samurai.

I take my books to work and brush up during the early evenings. Then I nap and have Shig Kodama wake me up every half an hour. At 4 A.M. I'm wide awake. *What if I don't get a bite? What if I have to keep brushing up forever? "He wen do all that studying for nothing!" they'll say. The way they laughed at Happy when he broke his jaw. Where's he now?*

"You'll get an offer sooner or later," Fujie says.

"It's already seven months four days!"

Then I wake one sweaty afternoon and see a brown envelope on the kitchen table. I tear it open and read the letter.

"I made it! I made it!"

"I told you so!" Fujie says.

"Yeah, you told me, Ma!"

It's a draftsman's job for the Army Airforce at Hickam Field, a dozen miles west of Honolulu. The subprofessional, grade 7 pays $2,300 a year. Even at 72 hours and time and a half, the plantation pays only $1,440!

I call my boxing buddy, Danny Lowe, who now works in personnel at Hickam. "Sure, old pal," he says, "we put you up anytime!"

Us boxers have a special bond.

I go to Mill Camp and ask Mr. Ichiro Kawai, our match-maker and Papa's best friend, "Will you tell my father that he cannot ask anything more from me? Even Takemoto *sensei* says since this is Hawaii ten years of filial piety is all a parent can ask."

"Why don't you tell him yourself?"

"Cannot! We'll fight. Will you? He'll listen to you."

He nods.

I stop by Kahana on my bagasse run and tell the old farts, "I did it all by myself. You people didn't raise a finger to help. In fact I did it in spite of you, thanks to Fujie."

Mama bows and bows and says, *"Kanshin, kanshin."*

"Are you making fun of me!?"

"I mean it. You *are* admirable," she says.

Papa says nothing.

Eleven years I spend on the plantation, but Shig Kodama is the only guy to wish me luck. "I give you credit! It took a lot of sweat and guts! You one real champ! . . ." he says.

I tell Fujie, "Bulaheads are real jealous buggahs. They don't want to see anybody get ahead."

I hire the Tengan taxi to take us to Kahului Airport.

"I'll send for you as soon as I can." I hug them all. I remind little Marcia, "Remember what Daddy said. Walk straight."

"Don't forget," Fujie says, "leave 'plantation talk' behind."

"Yah, yah."

I get butterflies the first day I report for work. This is the place where they pushed all the planes into the middle of the field and made them easy targets on December 7. They were so afraid of sabotage. Us Bulaheads were Fifth Column. Now they pass me from one office to another; I'm sworn in, photographed for my ID tag, lectured, and given pamphlets. They are all very polite, some of them nisei women. *I guess we can be trusted now after what the 100/442 did.*

The orientation lasts till 2. Then they take me to the drafting room and introduce me to George Wong, who's to be my supervisor. He takes me around the boards to introduce me to the 20 or so draftsmen. They're all local guys, mostly nisei. *What if I don't know enough? But anybody can draw a floor plan. Anybody can do details.* George assigns me a board and has me do lettering, dimensioning, and minor changes on other guys' drawings.

After a week I get to draw. I used to get a backache drawing on the kitchen table and in the cab of the Mack truck. Now I can stand at the drawing board. I keep knocking off one job after another. *Hell, I didn't need any correspondence school if this was all I was going to do.*

George takes me for coffee and says, "They wen tell you? You on probation for a year. You can get fired without a hearing during that time. After that, you get lifetime employment."

But I miss Fujie so much. I cannot relax without her. "I really miss you," I write her. Rent in Honolulu for a one-bedroom apartment when you can find one starts at $90. Even if I can find and pay for one, I'd need a car to commute to Hickam. Then I notice the empty barracks on the far end of the airfield. Can I rent one of them? I ask the big boss, Paul Saunders. He says several days later the Army will rent me a whole barracks for $20 a month. I send for Fujie and the kids. The electrical outlets are on one end, and the showers and laundry tubs are on the other end of the two-story building. A hallway runs through the middle the length of the building. Rooms are on each side, 60 in all. We take 2 rooms on the ground floor next to the outlets. Fujie cooks everything on hot plates. Nights are spooky with all the empty space. I worry while at work: what if some nut stumbles in?

Suddenly the veterans are bumping the nonveterans on the federal jobs. I worried so much about them getting killed, now I worry about them bumping me. *Why the hell they want a flunky job like this? They got the GI Bill, they can go to college.*

I take the family to Waikiki for a picnic every Sunday just to get away from the barracks. We bump into Peter Doi, Margaret's older brother.

"Hey, Pete, what you doing?"

"I'm attending UH."

"You going to be a draftsman?" It's just my luck to get bumped by him.

He sneers just like Mildred. "Nyyyaaaa, who wants to be a draftsman? I'm going to be a lawyer. I'm going to Harvard Law School after I finish UH."

"Go to it!" I say. He was drafted before the war and served as a translator in Australia.

"How is Margaret?" Fujie asks.

71

"Oh, she's married to Derek Omi of Omi Store in Kauai. She's the manager of the main store in Lihue. She has two sons. . . ."

I turn my deaf ear to him as he brags on and on.

"Say hello to her," Fujie says.

"You know why the Bulaheads brag so much?" I tell Fujie as we move off. "They don't talk much so they figure they have to talk big when they open their mouths."

"You know why you can't stand Peter?" she says. "He's a braggart like you, that's why."

"But I can back up my words. Besides, I'm not the jealous type. If anybody can break away from the pack, I tell um, 'Go to it!' Most of the guys, they sit back and hammer you if don't make it."

Many nisei vets are going to the mainland to become lawyers, doctors, dentists, and architects on the GI Bill. UH is still an agricultural college. It has only prelegal, premed, and prearchitecture. The plantations call the shots. They don't want guys becoming doctors and lawyers and leaving the plantations.

On September 1 over 25,000 sugar workers go on strike. In January last year there was a little-noticed article in the papers: the National Labor Relations Board ruled the National Labor Relations Act covered agricutural workers. Then in May the first-ever Democratic legislature passed the Little Wagner Act to include the field-workers on the sugar and pineapple plantations as "agricultural workers." Soon afterward the ILWU organized 11 of the 12 pineapple plantations and all 26 sugar plantations. Now the ILWU asks for cash instead of perquisites, a 65-cent per hour minimum, a 40-hour week, and a closed shop.

The Filipinos and Japanese are united now. They cannot use one against the other. In previous strikes, the planters evicted the strikers from their company-owned houses. Now there's nobody to do the evicting. The union has support from the dockworkers and the ILWU in San Francisco. The Big 5 import 6,000 workers from the Philippines. ILWU has its stewards and cooks sign up the immigrants before they land, withholding fresh fruits, and other treats unless they sign. The union brings in their own lawyers from San Francisco when no local lawyer would represent them.

The strike knocks the Tokyo trials out of the headlines. I

72

got out in the nick of time, but I'm not out. I'm still in the same boat. If we lose, we go back to the old plantation days. Back in 1940 Sears Roebuck opened a store in Honolulu. Matson Lines, owned by the Big 5 companies, refused to ship Sears' merchandise, which would compete with Liberty House, also owned by the Big 5. But Sears was big enough to hire its own ships.

I ask Yukio and Takako to keep me posted. The union gets a break when there's no rain. The fields are drying up. Management orders its *luna*s and field bosses to go irrigate the fields. In November the Political Action Committee comes through again: the Democrats win 15 of 30 Assembly seats, 14 of them endorsed by the ILWU. Hawaii has a population of 450,000, with 100,000 eligible voters, of whom 30,000 are ILWU members. If you count the spouses, it comes to at least 45,000 votes! For the first time in history Democrats take over Maui County.

In the old days any nisei who wanted to get elected had to run as a Republican. Even then he rarely got elected. Tom Hasegawa, a Pepelau boy, ran for county supervisor couple of times. He didn't have as many hula girls and musicians at his rallies, but he had a good line: "Remember Hasegawa as in 'Husky Guava!' No forget, vote for Husky Guava!"

"They'll take over. They already got the Democrats in their pocket," George Wong's haole supervisor says. "The ILWU is red. Hall and Bridges are card-carrying Communists."

"Cannot be," I say. "How come they endorsed Farrington?"

"Jack Hall has said so himself. He's not interested in party affiliation, only in those who'll do his bidding. So if the ILWU takes over, you'll be exchanging one dictator for another," he says.

At least they pay overtime, I almost say, but hold back. I got 7 more months on my probation.

As expected, the strike is real bitter at Frontier Mill. It's bound to be with an SOB like Jack Carlyle. Frontier has only 1,067 workers, 250 of whom live in Kahana. The *luna*s are the ones caught in the middle. *Luna* is the Hawaiian word for "upper." A plantation *luna* is a strawboss, who keeps a record of the gang's or individual's piecework production. When I won the Maui flyweight title for the third time in 1940, Nelson, the Kahana Camp overseer, offered me a *luna*'s job. I refused politely. I didn't know they'd offered one to Danny Lowe, too, who was lightweight champ. "I don't wanna be a stool pigeon," Danny said. *Luna*s wore safari hats, which the old farts called "kokusaka" (cock-sucker) hats.

The National Labor Relations Board cannot make up its mind whether *luna*s are management or labor. Carlyle orders them to irrigate the fields. They refuse except for Paul Nishino, who sneaks out one morning. The next morning pickets join hands and surround his house. Nelson comes for him and yanks him across the pickets, knocking down one of them. Right away the union files an assault and battery charge against Paul, then drops the suit when he joins the union.

Bill Toda tells Takeshi Tsuda, his brother-in-law, "Hey, no go walk through my yard. I no like scabs walking through my yard." Takeshi took shortcuts through Bill's yard. Takeshi is no scab, but refuses to join the union. Bill used to be one of the "drunk pile" during the war. Now he's the gung ho union rep for Kahana. Alcoholics are petty even after they reform. Bill even refuses to talk to his sister, who's married to Takeshi.

Takeshi's younger brother, Hideo, was a *luna* when he volunteered for the 442nd. He was a basketball star at Pepelau High. He was a year older and I knew him only slightly. After I started fighting, he'd come back to the dressing room afterward and congratulate me and Danny. Guys used to call Hideo and me the "*puka*-hunters." But he'd date only Portuguese girls. His mother warned him, "You'd better watch out, you're going to get one pregnant." "How come you no date a Japanee?" I asked him. "It's like dating your sister," he said. I only wish Mama was like his mother. Only 4 Japanese families in Kahana owned cars, and the Tsudas had the latest-model Chevy. All their sons were tall and 3 of them were *luna*s. Everybody looked up to them as the most successful family in Kahana.

Hideo wrote me a couple times, the first letter about their trip to Mississippi when they couldn't get off the train until dark. But the war is ancient history to the strikers, who now call him a scab.

"He's not irrigating the fields so he's not a scab!" I tell Fujie. "The guys too petty."

In fact not one of the 74 *luna*s at Frontier Mill is scabbing, but they're all ostracized.

The strikers boycott the Methodist church because Hideo's two brothers are pillars of the church. The strikers even boycott the pool hall because Freddy Andrade, another *luna*, manages it at night and on weekends. He's no scab either. How can you call not joining the union "scabbing?" The loud Takeshita brothers harass the kids of the *luna*s at Kahana Grade School and at the community bath: "Nya, nya, you faddah one scab!"

In Pepalau Masao Oda gets up every morning to picket his own house because his father, who runs the machine shop, goes to work. But the guy is management, not just a "yes-man" *luna*. He invented the sugar press, on which Frontier Mill owns the patent. Carlyle promised him his *luna* house for the duration of his life.

The Nishino fish market on Front Street lends Papa its sampan. They offer to pay him 50 percent of the catch, after expenses. He takes Yukio with him and brings home bagsful of *onaga, papio,* and *paka*. Before the war most of the fishermen were Japanese. They were so cutthroat they overfished the grounds. Martial law grounded them, and now fish is plentiful. Papa catches more than his plantation pay.

I write him, "Send me couple of good-sized *onaga* by air mail."

George Wong is crazy about fish. "I hate fish," I tell him, "but *onaga* is supposed to be the best. I'll get you some."

Papa sends me couple of *onaga*s and writes, "If the strike continues, I think I'll become a fisherman again. I'm the only one left who knows the old fishing holes."

Crazy asshole! I write back in big *katakana* phonetics, which is the only Japanese I know: "*Bakatare!* If you go into debt again, don't ask the children to help!"

"The old man nuts! I wash my hands!"

Good thing my tantrums don't bother Fujie. It's like water off a duck's back. She calms me down.

The strike gets ugly in Kahana. Joe O'Connor is the harvesting field boss. Somebody lets the air out of his truck tires by inserting twigs into the valve stems. Another time the strikers catch all the field bosses—Tony Gama, Louis Garcia, Kot Nakamoto, and Joe O'Connor—in the one-room plantation office and yell at them, "Thass the one, thass the one we gotta get! No scared him! He no boss no more!" "*Pilau* managah no more!"

"They only following orders," I tell Fujie. "Carlyle's the guy on top. He's the one to blame."

On November 16 all 26 plantations settle. The workers get 70½ cents to $1.38 an hour, up from a basic 43½ cents, a 48-hour week, but no closed shop. Rent, water, kerosene, medical, and hospitalization are no longer free. When the workers report to work on November 19, Jack Carlyle fires Mike Murai and 10 others, claiming they assaulted Mr. Crawford, who was irrigating a field. All the workers walk off again.

Carlyle is playing every card. For several months before the strike, Carlyle put an extra $100 in Mike's monthly pay envelope. Mike returned each "overpayment." Carlyle was a javelin thrower in the Olympics. During the 1937 Filipino strike he knocked out Kirito Ompad with one punch. He's 6'4" to Ompad's 5'5". At home we have a joke about Carlyle. Back in 1934 when we lived in Pepelau, Kiyo went to the machine shop next to the mill. Sadao Ono, or Anshan, who worked there, made him two shiny brass spears. Anshan used to take Kiyo and Joji spearfishing. Carlyle caught Kiyo walking out with the spears and dragged him back into the machine shop. "Is he the one? Is he the one? . . ." Carlyle dragged Kiyo to each of the dozen workers in the shop. Kiyo kept shaking his head. Carlyle went around again and again. Finally, after couple of hours he gave up and let Kiyo go. "Carlyle took the spears," Kiyo told Joji and Kite at the beach. That night Anshan came to the house with a fifth of White Horse and praised Kiyo to the skies. He would've been fired on the spot if Kiyo had fingered him. "Imagine a ten-year-old besting that *yatsu!* It's the talk of the machine shop!" Anshan crowed and crowed.

Carlyle threatens to turn the canefields into pasture land. "Let him!" the strikers say. The old farts are more gung ho than the niseis.

Miwa writes us that her brother-in-law, Tets Shiotsugu, was killed in Paris. He was one of the Kahana boys in the 442nd who never came home. Tets reenlisted and stayed in Europe. He was the third son of 7 boys and a football star in high school. He turned out for boxing after graduation. He had a good punch and figured that was all he needed. I kept telling him, "Boxing dif-

ferent from football, you all on your own." He KO'd several
guys, then got KO'd and quit. But I liked Tets the best among his
brothers. He was the only one who flew the coop. All the others
settled in West Maui. Their late father had asked that they not
move away because he'd be lonely in his grave. We can barely
scrape up $5 to send as *koden* incense money. He's the first death
from Kahana in the 100/442. "DNB," the papers will say.

Harry Bridges flies in on December 26 and gives a pep talk
at the Honganji Buddhist Church in Pepelau. The union is not
going to sacrifice anybody, he says.

"It's great," I tell Fujie. "At last we've got Carlyle by the
balls."

When Danny Lowe and Misae went back for Christmas,
the strikers gave him the cold shoulder. "Why?" I ask. He shrugs
it off. Danny's Chinese-Filipino father and Portuguese mother run
the single men's mess hall as a private business. The plantation
collects the monthly food bills for them directly from the pay-
checks of their customers, but there's no other connection. Besides, Misae's brothers and father are all union men. *Why they so
petty? The other camps not like that.* Then I realize: *in Pepelau all
the* lunas *live in Lunaville and not among the workers. But they
got along fine before the strike.* Then I remember Bill Toda saying,
"Know your class and be loyal to it." They're turning it into a
class war.

I have only $10 but I take the family into Honolulu to cele-
brate New Year's Eve. We walk around Waikiki, buy hats and
horns, and try to join in merrymaking. Marcia gets so tired, I carry
her piggyback. The left foot still points inward and she limps.
"Walk straight!" I keep scolding her. Danny Kenji is tired and
grumpy. Fujie too looks beat. *Maybe it wasn't such a good idea.
. . . But how can you spend New Year's Eve at the barracks?*

"Well, we wen celebrate. Les' go home," I say. But it's
only 11:00. We have 45 minutes till the next Hickam bus.

"Les' go eat saimin, I get enough for four small bowls."

We find a small Japanese restaurant near the Y.

The place is empty. I feel so low. Even with the strike the
people in Kahana will have a spread for New Years. *Good thing
the guys at the mill cannot see me now.*

We must've looked real sad. The bald-headed cook brings

out not saimin, but chicken teriyaki, pork *tonkatsu*, shrimp tempura, sashimi, and steamed rice.

"Mistake, mistake, I order four saimins!"

"On za hausu." His face lights up with a big Buddha smile.

"On the house?"

"*Hai*. Hap-pi New Ear."

"*Dohmo arigatoh.*"

Fujie sits up. "*Akemashite omedetoh gozaimasu!*"

"Haff hour more," he says.

Danny and Marcia stare at all the dishes.

"It's an omen. Our luck gonna turn around," I tell Fujie. "Happy 1947."

It happens right away. In the second week an apartment opens up at Hickam housing and we move out of the spooky barracks.

15

Civil Service

Carlyle gives in after New Years. He would've lost his crop if he stalled another month. He and the union agree to submit the status of the fired workers to the courts. Carlyle agrees the workers will get their old jobs back even if found guilty.

"Plantation job, now pretty good with the union. We get two weeks vacation and nine holidays," Miwa's husband, Hachiro Shiotsugu, writes.

"It's good for people like him and Papa," I tell Fujie.

George Wong feeds me more difficult jobs. But they're all the same. Floor plans, sections, details of barracks, PXs, officer's clubs, warehouses, and mess halls. The roofing, electrical, and plumbing don't vary either. The American Correspondence School had more complicated problems.

All the other draftsmen sit on stools and get backaches. I stand at the board. My back is fine.

"Hey, Steve . . ." George Wong says. I picked Steven as my American name when enrolling at the American Correspondence School. Back in the late '30s many high school kids were picking American names without legalizing them. It was like small-kid time when you said, "Call me 'Flash' and I call you 'Speed.' " Fujie called herself Carol, Takako Betty, Miwa Aileen. Joji was Georgie in Pepelau, and Kiyo became Morris when he joined the Army. I chose Steven because it was less common than Stephen. "Who this guy 'Winston Watanabe'?" We laughed when we first heard the name. "Oh, yeah, that's Takesaburo!? How come he wen pick Winston? Nobody in America named Winston!" Some names stuck, and others didn't. For me Steven meant I was leaving behind West Maui for a new identity in Honolulu.

"Hey, Steve, you working too hard," George Wong says at coffee one day. "The guys want you to slow down."

"Why?"

"You making them look bad."

"How come?"

"That's the way it is. The last guy who wen work too hard, they wen send him to Guam."

"You mean they punish you for working hard?"

"Something like that."

"I'm not really working hard, you know," I say, trying not to sound too haolefied. "I just fast. Besides, you supposed to pick up speed the fifth time you do the same thing. That's the way it was on the plantation. We got paid by piecework. You had to pick up speed because the plantation kept cutting the rates. Besides, I'm a plantation boy, not a city slicker. I not scared of work."

"Well, slow down, you way over the quota." I was putting out 2 sheets to the others guys' 1.

"You know," I tell Carol, "civil service is for old futts ready to retire. It's all seniority. George Wong, he's there fifteen years and he's still only a senior draftsman, grade 8. Grade 8 starting pay is only three hundred a year more than me. Only haoles in the top eschelon. Civil service just like the plantation."

"Civil service *is* just like the plantation."

"Yeah, *is* just like the plantation."

Goofing off is more tiring than working. But I don't wanna end up in Guam. I watch the other guys playing the "army game." Then I realize they're not goofing off, they're naturally slow. They draw every line, even the dimension and lettering lines, with a ruler or T-square; they measure off every 1/8″ and 1/4″ with the architect's scale. Then they dimension and letter carefully like they're creating a work of art. Drafting is already so labor intensive. It takes 50 to 100 hours to complete a single sheet of detailed working drawing. Why make it worse? All you want is the builder to understand you. You make it easier for him if you darken the important lines and lighten the others. Your drawing is a tool, not a work of art.

For the first time in my life I get so much time I don't know what to do. Work is only 10 minutes away, it's 7:30 to 4:00, half hour for lunch, 2 10-minute coffee breaks; I have the whole night off, the weekends, 9 paid holidays, and 2 weeks vacation after a year. I smoke a pack and a half just to kill time. But I have to lay low and act busy till my probation is up.

There are only 3 ratings in civil service—superior, satisfactory, and unsatisfactory. Your supervisor needs all kinds of paperwork to rate anybody "superior" or "unsatisfactory." So every-body gets an "S" or "Average." At the end of the fiscal year, man-agement says, "Use the budget or lose it." If you save the govern-ment money, they'll lop off that amount from the next year's budget. So there're all kinds of projects in June to spend the left-over money before the new fiscal year.

The job is all paperwork. We never get out to see the site or workers or clients. In fact we never get out of the office. When my one-year probation is over, I go over to where the specs writers are and chew the fat with them. But they act high *maka-maka* like the *luna*s. Hell, they're only one grade above us draftsmen. Peter Doi would do me a favor if he bumped me. The longer I stay here, the harder it's gonna get to get out.

"How come you never got out of civil service?" I ask George Wong.

"Nothing out there. Nobody building."

"What about before the war?"

"Worse. You hear of any Oriental making a living before the war?"

"Andrew Mori."

"Who else?" George's cousin Allen Wong in San Francisco got a degree from UC and a California license, but he ended up designing Chinese furniture for his brother's store on Grant Avenue.

"What should I do?" I keep asking Carol. "Civil service is a dead end. You don't learn enough to get a job outside."

We take the bus to Waikiki every Sunday just to get out of the base. Living on an Army base is worse than being stuck in Kahana. Most are haoles—GIs or government workers. George Wong and all the Bulahead and Paké draftsmen live in Honolulu. Danny Lowe too now lives in Honolulu. It's lonely for Carol.

"It's now or never," I tell Carol as soon as my probation is over. "If I don't get out now, I never will."

I call up Charles B. Ames of Ames and Horne, AIA, and ask him if I can work for them for love on Saturdays.

I make copies of 6 of my blueprints and take a day off. His office is on South King. He startles me. He looks just like Jack Carlyle. Bald, athletic, muscular, though not as tall as Carlyle's 6'4". He's in his mid-50s.

He looks over my prints. "What else?"

"That's all."

"What about specs?"

"The specs writers do it. It's all assembly line. But I know how to write specs."

"What are your credentials?"

"Beg your pardon?"

"What school did you attend?"

I mumble, "I dint go to college. I got a diploma in drafting from the American School in Chicago."

"What's that?"

"A correspondence school."

"So you want to work for love? Why?"

"That's the only way I can learn. All we do is office work. I know nothing about the outside. I figure you shouldn't pay me while I'm learning."

"Why me?"

"They say you and Andrew Mori are the only architects in Honolulu making a living."

"Why not Andy?"

"I don't like working for a Japanese."

He laughs. "Why not?"

"They oversupervise. They tell you, 'If you get time, go sweep the floor, eh?' "

He chuckles. "Okay, we'll use you. Jim will be in at ten next Saturday and show you what to do." He's a fast talker, sharp.

Jim Horne is the junior partner and the man on the board. He looks like Gary Cooper and says "Yep" and "Nope" like him. He's real happy. He supervises me for a couple of Saturdays, then he leaves me a load of work with instructions. I work every Saturday from 10 till 5, then buy *chow fun* to take home. It saves Carol from cooking and it's a treat for Danny and Marcia. "Walk straight!" I keep telling her. Her limp is hardly noticeable when she puts down her left foot squarely.

I spend most of my 2-week vacation helping Carol with Danny and Marcia. We take picnics to Kapiolani and Ala Moana. I work a couple of weekdays at Ames and Horne. *It's going to be a hot, long grind,* I keep thinking. Then there's a bombshell. A Bulahead named Ichiro Izuka publishes a pamphlet called "The Truth About Communism in Hawaii." Most of the guys he names, many of them nisei, are leaders in the ILWU. Just a week ago Gov.

Stainback gave a speech about the Communist menace in Hawaii. But the Tennesseean was so anti-nisei, anti-labor, anti-statehood and anti-everything that I tuned him out long ago. Now a week later John and Aiko Reinecke, who are mentioned in the pamphlet, are suspended from their teaching jobs. We have to sign affidavits at work saying we're not Communists.

"I think it's a plantation plot to bust the union," I say at coffee break.

"Yeah, but what he say is true. How come they no deny it?" Harry Ogawa says. He's a Honolulu boy like most of the draftsmen.

"But who paid for printing the twenty-nine thousand copies? I bet it was somebody in the Big 5."

"Why they so secret?" George Wong says. "That's what I don't like. Why they no can come right out and say, 'We Communist, we going organize the union.' "

"Cannot! In the old days you had to meet in secret to talk union. They kicked you out right away if they found out. You had to be there to know how the focking buggahs operate. They tried bribery, they tied a string to the pencil when you voted. If they win, they control the voting booth!" I lecture.

"But go look at Russia. Ten percent Communists control ninety percent of the population," George Wong says. "Same thing will happen in China if Mao takes over. It can happen here. All they gotta do is take over the leadership."

"But Jack Hall not a Communist. He wrote the rank and file and said so," I say.

"What about Harry Bridges? They trying deport him for being a Commie," Harry Ogawa says.

We go around and around, me against them. It's like arguing with the dumb dodos in Kahana. But then I think, *What if they're right? Nah . . .*

In December Chuck Ames offers to pay me $1.25 an hour for the 7 hours I put in on Saturdays.

16

Charles Ames

On May Day 1949 2,000 dockworkers go on strike. The *Honolulu Advertiser* publishes "Dear Joe" editorials (to Joe Stalin), bragging about how 2,000 ILWU men are tying up 450,000 people in Hawaii. Three hundred rich haole women form a Broom Brigade and picket the ILWU office at the waterfront. In August Gov. Stainback and the government seize the docks, but the West Coast is ILWU so the ships have to go all around to the East Coast. Stores run out of rice, bread, milk, and toilet paper. Businesses go bankrupt. But there's no end in sight and the public gets mad at the union. Living at Hickam, Carol shops at the commissary, where there's no shortage.

In September Russia explodes an atom bomb, which wasn't supposed to happen for another 10 years. Then Mao chases Chiang Kai-shek to Formosa. The longshoremen don't get parity with the West Coast, but both sides settle after 177 days.

A week after the strike ends, the 12 leaders of the Communist Party are found guilty of the Smith Act in New York. *What's the Smith Act? If it makes you guilty of being a Communist, how come the Hawaii Communists are not arrested?* Gov. Stainback and the *Advertiser* keep shrieking that the ILWU is a beehive of Communists, Hawaii will be next. I keep thinking about what George Wong said, about 10 percent kamikaze types taking over.

But that's the same thing they said about us Bulaheads before the war. We were the Fifth Column ready to take over as soon as the Japanese army landed. Now the Communists and the ILWU are ready to take over. But where's the Soviet army? How can anybody take over without an army?

I have so much time at work. I go over to the specs writers and architects and talk story. Most of them don't want to deal with a peon draftsman, but Ray Simpson, a vet in his late 30s, GS-11 or 12, is nice, besides being a good designer. Some are real lousy designers, especially the older guys. They were stuck in designing PXs and barracks for years and now can't hack it outside.

84

Ray comes into the office and invites me to coffee one day. "I can't take any more of this. I'm going back to Monterey to start my own business. Would you like to join me? I like your work," he says.

I'm so surprised I don't know what to say.

"We have to think of the children," Carol says. "They'll feel lost on the mainland. Besides, California hates *Nihonjin*."

I write Kiyo, who's studying Japanese history at Columbia. "Take it," he says. "The Big 5 has got Hawaii sewed up. All the opportunities are in the states. . . ." The guy always sounds so sure.

"We're barely out of the plantation, I don't see how we can make another jump to the mainland," Carol says. "Besides, we have to think of the children. I don't want them to go to a school where they'll be called Japs."

"Yeah." *It's too big a gamble. What if Simpson flops? He's a bachelor, he got nothing to worry about. What about all the expense of moving? And winter clothes and rent? I'm the big loser if he flops. So why I feel so flattered he choose me for his coolie?*

"My family comes first," I tell him.

When he comes to say good-bye I tell him, "I give you credit, civil service is for guys ready to retire. You cannot stay if you got any push."

In early January Alger Hiss is convicted of perjury. *Why perjury? If they cannot get you for something else, they use perjury?* A few weeks later the whole town buzzes about a movie MGM is planning about the 100/442, using 442nd vets living in L.A. The local vets, led by my old pal, Sunshine Kashima, protest, Hey, 100/442 was 2/3 Bulaheads! *Well, at least they using real Japanese. I'm sick and tired of Pakés and Yobos playing bucktoothed Japs. Maybe we'll finally find out what it was like.*

A week later Chuck offers me a full-time job at $2 an hour, which comes to about $4,160 a year. The Classification Act of 1949 boosted my pay to $3,950.

"That's only two hundred ten more than what I'm making. I get government housing, I can shop at the commissary. I need at least double that to live in town," I say.

He raises it to $2.25, $4,680.

"I get twenty-six days vacation and eleven days sick leave right now. In two years I'll get four thousand seventy-five," I say. He walks away. I never met a guy like him. He turns and walks away when he gets mad.

"But we have to think of Danny's and Marcia's schooling," Carol says. "Danny isn't happy with the school here. Besides, you have to go to night school for your high school diploma."

"You'd better tell Mr. Ames you accept his offer. He might take it back," Carol says.

"Naw, he needs me more than I need him." Jim Horne is the only man on the board and he's slower than the plodders at Hickam.

"I'll take it for two-fifty," I say the next time Chuck drops by.

"Two thirty-five," he says.

"With three weeks vacation?"

He sighs and jerks his head.

Is it a nod? I put on a *shibai* act, "Well . . . it's going to starve my family, but okay. . . ."

He looks away while he shakes my hand. $4,888. Even the top step of GS-7 gets only $4,575. The third step of a GS-9 is $4,850.

I go house hunting on Sundays. Rents are so high. It'd be cheaper to buy. Kaimuki is the best among the Japanese sections. It's a flat, dead-air pocket, but most of the woodframe houses sit on fee-simple land. Many houses in the other sections are on land leased for 99 years from the Bishop Estate. I find a run-down woodframe house on half a plot. Number 515 is the house on the street. A driveway leads to 515-A and its open 2-car garage. There's postage-stamp yard in the back. Eight thousand with $2,000 down is something I can raise. Bishop Bank and the Bank of Hawaii are the only banks and they don't loan to us poor Bulaheads.

"You think your brothers can loan me?" I ask Carol. "I'll pay them back at the four percent bank interest."

Seiji loans me $1,000, and Carol's other brother and Mrs. Nakama come up with $500 each. Papa don't have a pot to piss in.

I give my 2-week notice at Hickam and move into the one-bedroom house. The former owner built 3 cubbyhole bedrooms over the garage, which look more like the chicken coops Papa used to build with scrap lumber.

"This will be my first job," I tell Carol. I call up Mike Yasuda to help me. He's a carpenter (most of the carpenters are Bulaheads) who married Carol's sister, Mariko, back in '42, 4 months after our wedding. When Mariko got pregnant, her family was so mad nobody went to the wedding in Honolulu. Then when she was dying of breast cancer, everybody went.

Now Mike brings little Mary to the house and helps me on the weekends. We build a cosmetic *engawa,* a balcony and railing for the rooms over the garage, and a hipped roof with a small gable. "Give it some class," he says. We knock out a wall and install a glazed shoji panel in the $10' \times 11'$ dining room. A 6-foot counter separates the walk-through into the $8' \times 10'$ kitchen. Mike shows me how to build a Japanese "floating" ceiling. The $12' \times 1'' \times 1''$ strips of redwood look like they're holding up the beveled $12' \times 1' \times 1''$ redwood boards, but all the support is done from above. Vertical $1'' \times 3''$ boards are nailed to the rafters, and crosspieces at their feet are nailed to both the boards and strips.

"You one good carpenter," I tell Mike.

"You not bad wood butcher yourself," he says.

Carol baby-sits Mary and fixes us a big dinner. Mike's like me. He loves to eat, drink, and talk, and we kill off a fifth of J&B after every *pau hana.*

We finish remodeling in 8 weekends. I dig up $200 and put it in an envelope and shove it into his pocket.

"Hey, no need!" he says, giving it back.

"No, it's for Mary!"

"Caw-mon!" He tries to force it into my hands.

I pull my hands behind my back. "Listen, Mike, I'm pay-as-you-go, I no like owe you! Take it! Cost me five times more if I hire a carpenter! Is your J&B money."

Soon afterward Carol tells me she's pregnant!

I yell, "You supposed to use the diaphragm!"

"How can I put it on when you jump on me in your sleep!?"

"Why don't you put it on before you go to bed?"

"Every night!? Besides, it'll slip off!"

"Shit, I run down the old man for pooping so many babies! Now I doing the same thing!"

"It's only our third. Next time you have to let me know ahead of time."

"I bet you wen plan it all along!"

Damn these wahines. No matter how much you yell at them, they go right ahead and do what they want. How she expect me to get ahead? Just when I get a little ahead, she loads me with more expense. I go to the Columbia Bar and get plastered.

In April the House Un-American Activities Committee comes into town and they subpoena all the guys mentioned in Izuka's pamphlet. It's a circus. Jack Hall says he filed a non-Communist affidavit with the NLRB. So they know right away he's no longer a Communist. Was he ever one? they want to know. He takes the Fifth, and so do 38 others. Right away the papers call them the "Reluctant 39."

When the Democrats convene the next month, they squabble and squabble about being soft on communism. It's the same old plantation plot, divide and conquer.

I write specs most of the time as Jim hates to do them. I don't mind. That's the only way you learn material costs. They're written instructions, telling the contractor the materials, products, and workmanship required. It's an appendix to the drawings, which don't have the space for these notations. At Hickam the specs writers acted like their work was real tough. It's simple. You work from previous specs. You add new items, delete and modify others, but it's time-consuming because you have to check reference books, industry standards, and manufacturers' catalogs. It's as tedious as drafting.

The Korean war breaks out, but the big excitement in town is Hawaii's first title fight. Back in '47 Sad Sam Ichinose took Dado Marino to London to fight Rinty Monaghan for the world flyweight title. Dado got beat in 15 rounds. Monaghan retired, and now Dado is matched against Terry Allen of London for the vacant world title. Sad Sam guarantees Terry Allen $17,500 to fight Dado in Honolulu. Even in boxing you need money to get ahead. The Catholic Youth Organization fighters, Frankie Fernandez and Kui Kong Young, are top rated in *Ring Magazine,* but they cannot get title shots. Charlie Miller, who manages them, don't have that kind of money.

Danny and me, we scare up $2 each for the bleacher seats at the Honolulu Stadium. There's a radio blackout so the place is packed—reserved seats are from $3 to $8, and 10,000 general admission seats are $2. Dado and Allen look like midgets from where we sit. Dado is 34, Allen 26. Dado is a converted southpaw with power in both hands, but he cannot knock you out with one punch. He stays outside and boxes Allen the way he did me. Allen's got no punch and fights flat-footed. Dado's slowed down a lot, but he rocks Allen with left hooks and straight rights. Allen would have to KO him to win. It goes 15 rounds. The crowd roars as one when the referee raises his hand! My hair stands up and I get chicken skin.

We find a crowded saimin restaurant on South King.

As soon as we walk in, Danny says, "Boy, I never wen see so many Japs!"

Electricity zaps the room. Heads swivel.

Danny laughs. "Hey, I only kidding. I married to one Japanee. You ask my buddy here. Even my brudda married one Japanee."

"Yeah, he married to one Bulahead jes' like Jack Hall."

"Buddhahead!" somebody corrects.

"No, it comes from *boburahead*. It became Burahead, then Bulahead. Buddha had nothing to do with it. That's what Happy says."

Guys go back to eating.

"Any more news of Happy?" Danny says.

I shake my head.

Danny, like his brother Tommy, could pass easy for a haole, but they talk local.

"How old Dado?" Danny asks as we eat our saimin.

"Thirty-four. He three years older than me."

"You know, if not for Pearl Harbor, you and me, we punchy by now."

"Yeah, what a way to make a living."

Riding the bus back to Kaimuki, I think of the first time I fought Dado. I'm 3 inches taller than his 5'2½", and he didn't know I was a counterpuncher. He brought the fight to me and I floored him twice. But the next 2 times when it counted, Dado stayed outside and we exchanged jabs. A Honolulu boy fighting for Sad Sam's Japanese American Club was bound to win in a close fight. *But how else was I to fight him?* Sad Sam asked me to join his stable; I could fight as a bantam. *I'd be up against bangers like Manuel Ortiz and Kui Kong Young. Naw, Dado can keep his glory. Besides, now I smoke 2 packs a day and drink 3–4 beers. But I sure miss the roar of the crowd.*

The *Star-Bulletin* next day says Dado's take was only $1,500 to $2,000 out of a $42,673 gross from an attendance of 10,763. I'm glad I didn't turn pro.

Just when the UN troops have their backs to the sea, Gen. MacArthur does it again. He leapfrogs to Inchon, cuts off the Communists to the south, and takes Pyongyang, the North Korean capital. The troops will be home for Christmas, the papers say, as they move northward. He's ordered to stop but pushes to the Chinese border and suddenly Chinese troops swarm into North Korea. MacArthur is all for bombing the Chinese across the border. *Is it WW III?* The war grinds into a stalemate. Then MacArthur criticizes the UN and its policy of limited war, and Truman fires him.

Go for Broke premiers at the Waikiki Theatre. Kalakaua Avenue is jammed sidewalk to sidewalk. I think of the send-off Pepelau gave the 442nd volunteers. People cried. Now tears run down Carol's cheeks. Other faces are tear-stained. I sit Marcia on my shoulders when Van Johnson, Sunshine Kashima, and the other actors arrive. It's past 9 when we start back.

We finally get to see the movie when it comes to the Kapahulu Theatre. We like it so much we go back 3 more times. I cannot get over seeing Sunshine up there, bigger than life. We grew up together. He was packing me on his bike on Front Street and a car hit us and wrecked his bike, but we crawled out from under the car with only scratches and bruises.

Ames never works on the board. He does the program and design, and Jim and I do the working drawings and specs. "The first job of the architect is to bring in the job," Ames says. It pisses Jim. He tells me, "How can I bring in any job when I'm stuck on the board all day?"

Pidgin is rat-tat-tat quick. My good English has the same jerky rhythm and speed. "Beg your pardon?" "What d'you say?" Jim kept asking. Ames understood me, so it wasn't me but Jim. Was he hard of hearing? Then I figured it out. He's a slow talker because he's a slow thinker. My back-and-forth with Chuck is like a fast ping-pong match. With Jim it's like badminton. I wait and wait for him to finish his sentences.

Ames designs a $500,000 colonial home in Manoa for Keith Reynolds, heir to the Alcoa fortune. He adds $35,000 to the $50,000 fee. "You realize he makes money every time you drink beer out of a can? You have to soak the rich. They don't know how to spend their money," he says.

I admire the guy, but Jim don't think it's funny. Their partnership reads: Charles B. Ames, AIA, and James E. Horne, AIA, but it cannot be 50/50. He treats Jim like he was just another draftsman.

"Are you finished already? How did you do that?" Jim said the first time I finished a project. "Are you sure that's accurate?" He got up from his board and checked my lines with a ruler. "I can scale by eye. I don't need a ruler to plot every line," I said. "You got a natural talent, Steve," he said.

Jim is mid-40s, twice divorced, a regular ladies' man. He takes longer lunches and comes back smelling like a gin mill. He'd sit on a project for days and give it to me a couple days before the deadline. When we work together he lets me do all the work, then takes over when it's nearly finished.

"Shit, it's the plantation all over again!" I bitch to Carol.

"Why don't you tell Mr. Ames?"

"I'm not a stool pigeon!"

I start night school at McKinley. Mr. Skinner says I already have more math than I need. All I need is junior and senior English and social science.

One day Chuck hands me some designs. "I want you to do this yourself. Don't give any of it to Jim. He's too slow."

Several months later Jim quits to open his own office. He asks me to join him at $2.50 an hour.

"Jim's offering me two-fifty," I tell Ames.

"I'll give you two sixty-five."

"Two seventy-five."

He jerks as if to walk away but nods, looking away. *Why he cannot come out and say what's on his mind?* Instead he talks with body English. *All New Englanders like that?*

My $5,720/annum already passes George Wong and the highest step of GS-9, which is $5,350.

"You know, I think I make a good labor negotiator," I brag to Carol. Ames has connections. He did the Winterthur Museum in Delaware for Francis duPont. They say he's one of the best "Colonial" men in the country. As well known as Ed Stone is in his field. Jim is a mediocre designer and his only contacts are his drinking buddies.

"Hey, you no scared working for one *mahu?*" "Hey, he no goose you when you on the board?" "You better watch out, no go turn your back to him," the guys at the Columbia kid me. I must've been the only draftsman in town who didn't know Charles Ames is a homosexual.

Ames' jokes never made sense before.

"You smell like mothballs," he whispered once, his hand on my shoulder. "How d'you get between his legs?"

"Come again?" I looked up from the board.

He cracks up, doubling over. "How d'you get between the moth's legs?" he shrieked.

"Come again?"

He laughed so hard he choked.

"What's so funny?" I said.

"What's this 'Come again?' " he said, coughing, red in the face.

"That's what we say instead of 'Beg your pardon?' "

He finally stopped giggling and said, "Where were we?"

"Mothballs," I said.

"Yeah, you smell like mothballs. How d'you get between his legs?"

"I don't get it."

"You're killing the joke, Steve. The moth got balls between his legs. You smell like mothballs, so how d'you get between his legs?"

"Dat joke or what?"

There was another joke I never got. A man went into an

antique store and picked up a hairpiece. "What is it?" he asked. It's a merkin. What's a merkin? A false pubic hair piece for wahines. It was popular in Elizabethan times when women were bald down there. "I'll take it," the man said. "Shall I wrap it?" the proprietress said. "No, I'll eat it right here," the man said, and Chuck cracked up while I waited for the punch line.

He might be a *mahu,* but his clients are the Dillinghams and Hagens and the haole elite of the territory.

Korea is a stalemate. Cease-fire talks begin in July. One by one the Hawaii KIAs appear in the papers. West Maui has 8, none of whom I know—a Chinese, a Hawaiian, 2 Filipinos, and 4 Bula-heads. They're integrated now. The 100/442 was lucky to be seg-regated. Every death counted for something. Now the poor guys are lost in the shuffle in an unwinnable war.

Just when I think the red scare has died down the FBI arrests Jack Hall and 6 others. The red-baiters scream when Judge Metzger reduces their bail from $75,000 to $5,000.

Then Japan lucks out again. The Tokyo trials are cut short, the peace treaty signed, and the rest of the war criminals released. The man at the top, the emperor, gets off with a slap on the wrist. They must figure most of the atrocities were committed against the Chinese, who're Communists now, and Japan is to be the so-called bulwark against communism in Asia.

After Chrys Fumiko is born, we fly to Maui on a Saturday for Carol's younger brother's marriage.

The next day Miwa invites us to the Shiotsugu family reunion. After Tets died in Paris, there are 6 boys left, and they all get together every weekend at their widowed mother's house and play penny-ante *hana fuda.* Their wives and children have their own games.

"Oh, Toshi-chan, long time no see, eh? I hear you doing well, yeah?" Miwa is always so upbeat.

I take off my shoes and go inside and right away I'm boil-ing mad. They have a pecking order, and Miwa, married to the youngest son, is lowest on the totem pole. She and the other 3 wives serve the men and she takes orders from everybody.

I follow Minoru out to the veranda. He tried to bully me

when I worked as his helper. Then he tried to *boto-boto* me when I called his bluff.

"Hey, Minoru, how much you making now?"

"Plantation work now one good deal. The union wen change everything," he says.

"So how much you making?"

"Dollar-ten an hour."

"That's all? How long you been working here?"

Miwa pokes her head out the screen door and goes back in.

"Twenty-three years."

"And you making only buck-ten an hour?"

"Yeah."

"You been working all those years and you making only buck-ten?"

He says nothing.

It's like pulling teeth. "Buck-ten! Phew!" I say to break the silence.

Finally he bites. "Yeah, how much *you* making?"

"Two seventy-five an hour."

Miwa looks out again to make sure we're not fighting.

"Yeah?"

"Yeah. It take you two and a half years to make what I make in one year! And I did it in less than five years."

I feel so good I go inside and join the party. "Hey, you guys joined up with the Commies yet? Jack Hall—"

"We no care if Jack Hall one Communist, we stick with him. Because of him the bosses no can yell at us no more!" Shiro says.

"Who you choose, Carlyle or Jack Hall!?" Jisky says.

"Jack Hall quit the Communists," Hachiro says.

"Even if he one Commie we stick with him!" Shiro says.

"He wen give us one living wage," Hachiro says.

"You one stool pigeon or wat!?" Jisky says.

I laugh. "Hey, I just kidding."

Miwa breaks into a big smile.

"Since you're so successful, can you board Tsuneko so that she can attend the University of Hawaii next year?" Mama asks me.

"Cannot! I'm still paying off my loan to Fujie's brothers! Ask Kiyo or Joji!"

"But you're the only one in Honolulu."

"Cannot! I got too many expenses!"

"But everybody says you're successful."

"I'm barely surviving! I made the back of my house into a rental so I can get more income!"

Then she asks Carol, "I spoke to Toshio, but he wouldn't listen. Could you board Tsuneko so that she can attend the university? We'll pay you twenty-five dollars a month. We won't ask for anything more."

When Carol tells me, I explode, "Why didn't you refuse! I already told her no!"

I run down Pigpen Avenue.

"I work for you for ten years! You couldn't even send me to high school! I had to go to night school for my high school diploma! Now you want to unload Tsuneko on me! CANNOT! Twenty-five a month is not enough! I have to help Fujie's brothers and their children first! Do you know why!? They loaned me two thousand so that I could buy a house! I didn't get a cent from you! Not one cent! I'm washing my hands of you and Papa! I was *oya kohkoh* for ten years! That's enough! I paid off your debt!"

"You didn't pay off the debt. Kiyoshi did with his Army pay."

"*Bakatare!* Army pay is fifty dollars! How can he pay off six thousand dollars on fifty a month!? He had to crook!"

"What do you mean?"

"He had to cheat. Half of it was dishonest."

"I don't know what you mean."

"Look at your other son. He's a crook like grandfather."

"Who? Joji? What did he do?"

"He used to be gambling partners with Hiroshi Sasaki."

"Well, he's in Germany now."

"And running a black market. He keeps asking me to send him cigarettes."

"Why do you hate Tsuneko so much?"

"I don't hate her! My family comes first! I told you over and over! Educate the boys...." *I'm away 4½ years, but everything's the same! She press a button and I spew like a volcano!*

Carol calms me down.

"Why the hell she brings it up now!? Ann's graduation is a year and a half away."

Dado Marino has a rematch with Terry Allen at the Honolulu Stadium in November. Danny and I stay home. Dado wins in 15 rounds but only 8,813 show up, grossing $26,009. Both fighters get 25 percent of the net, or $1,659 each. Then a month later Sad Sam matches him against Yoshio Shirai, the Japan champ. Dado beat him in Tokyo last spring so Sad Sam must think it's a cinch. But Dado just fought 15 rounds! At 35 he needs rest! Only 2,766 show up, paying $6,547.65. Shirai, 27, floors Dado 6 times till Sad Sam stops it in the seventh round. Good thing it was a nontitle fight.

17

Jack Hall

Chrys cries so much we see one specialist after another. Marcia needs braces. Girls are nothing but expense. Good thing Carol cuts out coupons and watches for sales. I can barely make the payments to her brothers. Termites are eating up my house. They fly out of the infested walls at night.

After attending classes 3 nights a week for 9 months I get my high school diploma from McKinley. Ames lets me take off twice a week to take classes at UH spring semester. On the first morning I see Peter Doi on the bus. He waits for me to get off.

"What're you doing here?" he scolds.

"I'm taking a course."

"As a freshman?"

"No, unclassified."

"In what?"

"Structural engineering."

"Why?" He acts like he's already a lawyer.

"I work for an architect."

"I'm a senior now. Next year I'll be going to Harvard Law School. Imagine, I'll be the only Harvard graduate out of Kahana, probably all Maui. I'm planning to go back to Maui and run for county supervisor. After that the Senate. . . ."

He brags-brags-brags. "Yeah?" I say, or "Go to it."

I cannot shake him off. He waits for me every time. When I get off first and take off, he comes running after me and walks me right up to my classroom, even when his class is way across campus. His sister called me a "garbage collector." Now it's his turn. He's graduating in a year and I'm not even a freshman. We're the same age. He worked 4 years before going to high school; then he got drafted as soon as he graduated in 1941 and spent the war in Australia, translating captured Japanese documents. So we're both playing catch-up, but he's way ahead of me. He acts friendly, but it's his way of rubbing it in. Whenever I'm late, he waits to see if I'm on the next bus. Then I start counting—he should've graduated 2 years ago if he started in '46.

"How come you not graduated already?" I ask him next time he waits for me.

"I had to work. GI Bill is not enough."

In May Dado goes to Tokyo to put his title on the line. Shirai hires Richard Chinen to coach him. Chinen got cited for bravery as a medic in the 442nd. I fought him twice before the war, winning and then losing. We were both counterpunchers so we waited for the other guy to lead. So we just kept dancing and exchanging jabs. *What's the matter with Sad Sam? You fight in enemy territory only if you know your man will knock out the other guy.*

Shirai beats Dado 7 rounds to 5 with 3 even. But the gate is $120,000! Wow! I only hope Dado gets a big cut. Back home Sad Sam says he got no alibis, Dado was sluggish.

We get a piece of good news in June. Kiyo gets a B.A. from Columbia.

"He broke the mold!" I tell Carol. "I bet he's the first Oyama even in Japan to get a college degree!"

He majored in Japanese history and sends us a Zen riddle of *kanji*s on a 6″ × 6″ card: 矮錐

"What it mean?" I ask Carol, who knows *kanji*.

"It's a visual puzzle. You see the *kuchi hen* is used with each character.

She writes it out: 吾唯足知 "*Ware wa tada tari wo shiru.*
" 'I know only what's enough'? Or 'To know what's enough is enough.' Something like that."

"How can you get rich if you think like that?"

Ann graduates from Pepelau High, and Papa writes Takemoto *sensei,* who now runs the Nuuanu Methodist Church. Boarding at the church costs $100 a month. Papa makes $125 a month as ditchman.

"What are we going to do about Tsuneko's education?" Mama writes me.

"Look at her!" I yell at Carol. "She got the nerve to ask what am I gonna do about it! Like it was *my* responsibility!"

I write her in big *kana:* "LET HER WORK HER WAY THROUGH COLLEGE! SHE'LL GET MARRIED ANYWAY!"

Mama writes again, "All her classmates are going off to college. Tsuneko will feel left out if she cannot go to college. ..."

Congress passes a new law allowing Asians like Papa and Mama to get naturalized.

Carol finally persuades me to let Ann stay with us to attend UH for $30 a month room and board.

"That's not even half of what it'll cost!"

Damn old farts! They're the reason I grind my teeth in my sleep.

Then in August Kiyo writes them from Washington, D.C. and says Ann can live with him and attend George Washington University. He's working at a government medical library, cataloging Chinese and Japanese medical books the U.S. Army acquired in Japan.

"You lucky, you catching all the gravy," I tell Ann when I drive her to the airport. "Mama and Papa didn't even let me finish high school. I had to go to work when I was sixteen and I worked ten years and during that time they gave me only five dollars a month *kozukai*. ..." I give her an earful.

A month later Georgie gets a discharge from the Army and comes home with his Austrian wife, Gertrude Beck. He broke up with Evelyn Kikawa 2 years ago when I wrote him Papa still said he would have to leave West Maui in shame if he married Evelyn. *Shit, I not your messenger!* I felt like telling him. Besides, why did he have to ask Papa's permission all the time? Why didn't he just marry Evelyn if that's what he wanted and to hell with gossip!

I ask him to stay with us, but he checked in at Kobayashi Hotel already. We take them to Halekulani for dinner.

"What you gonna do?" I ask him.

"I'm going to work at Johns Mansville and go to school at night," he says.

"George is going to become an architect," Gertrude says. She has flaming red hair.

"Go to it," I say.

"I want to beautify the face of the earth and leave something for posterity," he says.

"Yeah?"

"I'm the one who will be making the sacrifice," Gertrude says in her thick accent. "George will be working nights and going to school in the daytime. I won't be seeing him. But it's worse if he don't finish college, yeah?"

"Yeah, all us Oyamas got two strikes against us. We cannot make it if the wives don't pitch in. Papa was a failure. He pooped seven kids when he cannot support three. He had no ambition. He—"

"You're too hard on him," Georgie says. "If he succeeded, he'd have taken us back to Japan, and you'd probably ended up a kamikaze."

"Not me." The guys always comes out of left field.

I tell Carol later, "It's gonna be hard for Georgie."

Haole wives are like nisei girls who're real pretty. They think they can cash in on their looks. Haole girls cash in on their skin. They don't even have to be pretty. At the office, Ted Taketa's mainland haole wife runs him ragged, calling him all the time. Couple guys from West Maui came home with mainland haole or German wives. Before the war all the waitresses were Oriental or Hawaiian. Now there're many mainland haole waitresses. Before the war the only haole girls were daughters of the plantation bosses, and they didn't know how to boil water. Now people say of the hardworking, undemanding haole war bride, "She's a good wife." You never hear people say that of a nisei wife. It's taken for granted she's a good wife.

Georgie was stationed at Camp Cook before his discharge. He and Gertrude couldn't find anybody who'd rent to them in the nearby towns. "Even the gas stations had signs, 'No Japs or Krauts wanted,' " Gertrude said. They stayed in a motel in the Mexican section of Santa Maria till they met Arnold Kojima, a nisei who lived in Pocomo. Arnold rented them a house and offered to sell Georgie a lot for $800. The valley had been full of Japanese farmers before the war, but only Arnold came back. The rest lost their land when they got sent to the camps. Georgie says he's going to build a house on the lot while working for Johns Mansville at night. The valley is surrounded by limestone hills, and Johns Mansville Co. sucks out the limestone and makes a powder called celite.

I'm happy he's leaving. He'd have fallen in with his old

pal, Hiroshi Sasaki. Hiroshi is now a professional gambler and preys on passengers on cruise ships. Couple of times the captain put him ashore when the players complained about his cardsharping. He and his syndicate still run Nevada-style crap games in the plantation camps on Sundays, and they take bets on all sporting events. He must pay the cops, who leave him alone.

Georgie and Gertrude stay a week in Kahana and convince Betty and Yukio to go with them to Pocomo. Yukio would go first and help Georgie and Gertrude build their house. As soon as they finish it, Betty and their three children would join him. They'd all live with Georgie and Gertrude while they build Yukio's and Betty's house. Georgie would buy the 2 adjoining lots and sell one of them on credit to Yukio.

I write Betty, "I'll get Yukio a carpenter's job in Honolulu if you want to leave Kahana. I know some contractors. Georgie is all mouth. You cannot trust him . . ."

What scares me is there'll be only Miwa and me left to look after the old farts in their old age.

"We want to leave Hawaii," Betty writes back. By then Georgie, Gertrude, and Yukio are in California. They flew out without stopping by.

The Democrats squabble so much the Republicans capture both territorial houses again in '52. The next day the trial of the Hawaii 7 begins. Back at the House Un-American Activities Committee hearing in April '50 I didn't pay much attention to Jack Kawano, one of the Reluctant 39. But he was unlike the other 38 because he answered the first part of "Are you or have you ever been a member of the Communist Party?" with "I am not a Communist," then refused to say anymore. Jack Hall quit the Communist Party too, but took the Fifth all the way after saying he filed a non-Communist affidavit with the NLRB. I thought that was the end of that after Judge Metzger threw out the contempt charges against the 39. But in July '51 Kawano went to Washington, D.C. and testified in secret before the HUAC. Chuck Mau went with him to hold his hand and Ben Dillingham paid for his airfare and hotel. The following month the FBI arrested the Hawaii 7. Now 14 months later all these behind-the-scene shenanigans come out in the trial.

It's a good thing Chuck Ames and I don't talk politics.

Many of the red-baiters are Chuck's clients. The cluster of federal, territorial, and city buildings are less than a mile away from our office on South King. It's like sitting at ringside. On days when he likes the testimony, Chuck pores over the papers in his inner office and he glides when he walks.

Izuka is the third prosecution witness. He rehashes his "The Truth About Communism in Hawaii" pamphlet. I'm sure glad I didn't waste two bits on it. The prosecution brings in their big-gun professional witnesses from the states. They were former bigwigs in the Communist Party like Budenz and could testify about the Communist conspiracy. It's dull, like watching 2 counter-punchers. Finally we come to the main event: Kawano. He's not a small potato trying to make a name for himself. He was one of the original organizers and leaders, a heavy hitter. In direct testimony he repeats what he said to HUAC in '51. The fireworks start when Gladstein cross-examines him. Kawano says Chuck Mau, Mitsu-yuki Kido, Ernest Murai, Dan Inouye, Sakae Takahashi, and Ernest Heen encouraged him to go to Washington to testify to the HUAC. He got "loans" of over $8,000, secured by Mau, from Kido, Murai, and Capitol Investment to set up a liquor store, to be paid back if he made money. He admits he hates Jack Hall only because Hall was a Communist. He admits going to the CIO to try to replace Hall. He admits the '49 longshoremen's strike was over wages and had nothing to do with the Communist party.

Kawano is bitter that Jack Hall got appointed regional director instead of him. But he's the silent, sincere samurai type. No matter how great you are behind the scenes, you need *shibai* and *ho'omalimali,* you need to be a talker and public speaker to be a leader up front. He's not in Hall's class. And now he lets these new Democrats use him. They want to prove they're not soft on communism. He don't realize once you're branded a stool pigeon, you're finished.

Jack Hall quit the Communist Party 3 years ago and the prosecution knows it. That's why Hall wants a separate trial from the other 6, who are probably still Communists. One of them, Koji Ariyoshi, publisher of the *Honolulu Record,* was an interpreter like Kiyo, but he served in North China and became a friend of Mao Tse-tung. The prosecution knows Hall won't turn STOOL PIGEON and say he's no longer a Commie so they feel they can lump him with the 6, including John Reinecke, Ariyoshi, and Charles Fuji-moto, who says openly he's the party chairman in Hawaii. The Big 5 are out to crush the union by convicting Jack Hall for being something he's not. Communism is just a ploy. None of the 6 others are worth a trial.

The jurors sat for 32 weeks, but need only 16 hours, 17 minutes to find all guilty. A day later Julius and Ethel Rosenberg, convicted for being wartime Communist spies, are executed. On July 3 the anti-ILWU judge gives the Hawaii 7 the maximum: 5 years in jail and a $5,000 fine, and he ups the bail to $15,000. *If Jack Hall goes, the union is pau. All Hawaii will be a plantation again.*

Chuck is chatty and all smiles, while I feel like spitting. The battle comes right into our office. *White man's burden,* Happy said.

What the hell is the Smith Act? If they can throw you in jail for being a Communist, how come all the others not in jail? They convicted the 12 in New York under the same Smith Act.

I take my first trip to the main library to look up the Smith Act. This "Alien Registration Act of 1940" was passed to deport Harry Bridges. Teaching overthrow of the government was con-spiracy. *It's like the Japs making "Dangerous Thoughts" a crime. No wonder lawyers are crooked, the laws are crooked. They for snagging not crooks but political enemies!*

Jack Hall calls work stoppages and the union holds testi-monial dinners for him. Stainback and the *Advertiser* howled when Judge Metzger reduced each bail to $5,000. Now they scream: Jack Hall, the "convict," is thumbing his nose at them!

Then Carol says she's expecting! "Chrys needs a compan-ion," she says, like I don't count.

Just when I take a step forward, I get pushed back. "Shit!"

"It's our last."

The cease-fire talks in Korea finally produce a cease-fire and a Demilitarized Zone on July 27.

In August Mama leaves for Japan. We all chipped in for her trip. It's urgent since her mother is 82. She was 44 when Mama last saw her, 38 years ago. It's a boat trip and her group of 50 will tour all Japan for a month. Then she'll spend the second month with her family in Fukuoka.

"Ah," Mama says when I pick her up at Honolulu Harbor, "even if mother dies tomorrow I'll feel at peace. I said my good-bye."

The photos she brings back show her walking on air. All her relatives are in their best kimonos, faces beaming.

Carol's mother's relatives are all dead.

Back in '47 Danny and I used to go to the Civic Auditorium to watch a local boy, Carl "Bobo" Olson, fight. He fought main events at 18. He left for the mainland and fought out of his new home base near San Francisco. "You watch, he'll be back driving a cab," Danny said. He had a good punch, but wasn't fast. There were too many good middleweights—Zale, Cerdan, LaMotta, Robinson. I didn't think he'd go far. He fought Sugar Ray in an American Legion event and got KO'd in the thirteenth. Then Robinson retired and suddenly all the good middleweights were gone. In October 1953 Bobo decisions Randy Turpin for the vacant crown, and Hawaii celebrates its second world champ. *Ring Magazine* votes him "Fighter of the Year."

"Dado and Bobo putting Hawaii on the map," I tell Danny.

"Yeah, now he can buy a *fleet* of cabs," Danny laughs.

18

Bloc Voting

In February 1954 the Central Bank of the Pacific opens for business at North King and Smith. It's locally owned and run by *issei* businessmen and nisei vets. Ever since the Japanese banks were shut down after Pearl Harbor there were no banks for Bulaheads. The Bank of Hawaii and the Bishop Bank are haole banks with a haole staff for haole clients. Mr. Ueda, who owned a small grocery store in Palama, went to them to borrow $2,000 to buy some rice. They turned him down even when he had a successful business. That's when Ben Moriyama and other vets said, "Hey, we go form our own bank!" Opening day the city and county of Honolulu and the territory of Hawaii each deposit $100,000. Carol has to wait in a long line to open our account. Right away the Bishop Bank and Bank of Hawaii start hiring nonhaole clerks.

In April Bobo Olson decisions Kid Gavilan in Chicago and earns over $116,000. He's only 24! *He can own all the cabs in Hawaii!*

I can barely keep afloat on the $833 a month Ames pays me. I'm still paying off the 2 Gs I borrowed to buy the house. A fourth kid is due in 3 months. I borrow 2 Gs from the Central Bank of the Pacific to fumigate the house. They cover the whole house with plastic so we have to eat and sleep in a hotel for 4 days.

Joe Correa, a cop, lives *mauka* to me, and Mrs. Leong, *makai.*

"You know what you doing?" Joe says, and laughs. "The termites going underground and going come to my house."

"Naw. They no go *mauka.* They go *makai.*"

Mrs. Leong says, "I going fumigate my house next year and I going send the termites back to you."

We make it back on time without causing Carol too much worry. In May Carol has a boy. We name him Gerald Hiromi. It's silly to give him a Japanese name. Nobody, not even Papa and Mama, call the grandkids by their Japanese names. Queens Hospital charges us $100. I pray nobody gets real sick. I'd lose everything. One good thing the ILWU did for the workers: medical care and hospitalization are no longer free, but they're covered by a plan the union won for them.

Carol looks so beat. She needs a vacation. When school lets out, I write the old folks I'm sending Danny and Marcia to them for the summer. Couple years ago I'd sent Danny by himself. The older guys scared him to death. *"Chimpo katchi, chimpo katchi,"* "Cut your prick, cut your prick," they chased him make-believe. Kahana guys are real crude. Danny is 10 now and no longer a new face.

"You don't deserve it, but you'll have a chance to know your grandchildren," I write, and enclose a check for their board, including a round-trip taxi fare to Kahului Airport.

Kaimuki gets so hot in the summer. I buy a '51 Chevy just to get out. I drive Carol, Chrys, and baby Gerald to windward Kailua. It becomes a Sunday ritual. The water is aqua blue. We swim, picnic, and forget about sweltering Honolulu for 6 hours.

"I no wanna go back," Danny says when I pick them up in August.

"Why?"

"Grandpa, he real mean to Scott."

"That's the way he was to me!" I say.

The 4 of them had played together every day. Scott, 10, Danny, 10, Marcia, 8, and Miwa's girl, Maxine, 10. One day they played follow the leader and jumped across the 3-foot sewage/irrigation ditch. Marcia, with her gimpy leg, fell into the ditch, and Scott caught hell from Papa. But the worst time was when they all went to gather snails at the reservoir and came home at dusk, their clothes all wet. Papa flung the pail of snails and whacked Scott across the face.

"That's what he used to do with me!" I say to Danny and Marcia.

"But Grandma wen go gather all the snails and we had them for supper," Marcia says.

Danny has Carol's softness whereas Marcia's a fighter like me.

Many nisei vets who went to the mainland for their law degrees are comig home to practice, some going into politics. They come into Kaimuki and hold coffee klatches in private homes. "It's time for a change. We need to break the monopoly of the Big 5 and redistribute the land. Everybody deserves a share of the pie," they say. No hokey stuff like the hula girls and "Vote for Husky Guava." Before the war the older niseis said we should stand back and not scare the haoles and have them accuse us of bloc voting. Now these young guys say *"Tanomimasu"* or *"Okage sama de,"* even if it's the only Japanese they know. Every nisei knows what it means: "I appeal to you," or "I am what I am because of you." Niseis are now 35 percent of the registered voters in the territory.

I never saw Peter Doi after June '52. I figure he graduated and went on to Harvard. So I almost jump out of my shoes when I see somebody who looks like him. He crosses the street and turns the corner. I run after him. *"Nyaa . . . who wants to be a draftsman?"* I still see that sneer. *How come he and Margaret so bossy and all the younger brothers so nice?*

"Hey, Peter, you a lawyer yet?" I run up to him.

"Naw, not yet," he says, and keeps walking.

"So when you gonna go to Harvard Law School?"

"Later."

"Yeah, when?"

"Some time."

"You got enough grade points for Harvard?"

"Sure."

"So how come? I been bragging to all my friends you the first Harvard graduate from Kahana. You making me a liar?"

He laughs and walks faster.

I keep right up. "So what you doing now? You working for a lawyer?"

"Something like that."

"Like what?"

"V.A."

"That's federal?"

"Yeah."

"What grade?"

"GS-9."

"What step?"

"Third."

"That's what? Fifty-two hundred?"

"Yeah."

He keeps moving off, but I'm right on top of him.

"Wow! You know how much I making?"

"How much?"

"Ten Gs! Double of what you make!"

He's practically running now.

I yell after him, "Lemme know when you pass the bar! I looking for a lawyer!"

I crow to Carol that night. "I know now what they mean when they say, 'Money talks.'"

"You're so vindictive."

"I jes' wanna get even."

Bloc voting is a hot topic. The papers write about it everyday. Back in the late '40s a Bulahead ran for supervisor in Honolulu on a "Vote Japanese" platform. The guy was an embarrassment. These new guys are different.

The Columbia Bar is the watering hole for the nisei draftsmen and contractors. The architects go to the more upscale Waikiki Grand, but Dick Kawasaki, AIA, USC, and Lenny Imai, Univ. of Wisconsin, landscape architect, come slumming. Both are 10 years younger than me but they can suck um up straight whiskey with the best of us.

"You think there's gonna be bloc voting?" I ask at the bar.

"If you grow up on the plantation, you one Democrat. It's not bloc voting," Dick Kawasaki says.

"The Irish, the Italians, every minority race that got up the ladder did it by bloc voting," Lenny says.

"Japanee not one minority. We thirty-five percent, same as the haoles," Dick says. "So it's haole Republicans versus Buddhahead Democrats. They the ones who vote in blocs."

"It's Bulahead, not Buddhahead," I correct him.

Ames was all smiles when they convicted Jack Hall. Then he looked annoyed when nothing came of it. *Is it because he's a mahu?* Once in a while I catch him flipping his wrist or walking up the steps holding up his pants legs like it was a skirt. Looks funny because he's burly and bald like a truck driver. We used to call the guys wahines who were real girlish, but we never persecuted them. We knew their brothers and sisters. Ames drops in 2–3 times a day when he's having me work on his designs. I know how he thinks, so I don't have to stop and ask him for every little omission. He probably pays me more than any head draftsman in town. But compared to what the office makes and and how much of the work I do, it's peanuts.

College graduates need 3 years' experience before they can take the architects' exam. Without college I need 12 years. Hawaii has no reciprocity. The board flunks 85 percent of the applicants every year in order to protect the local architects. No matter how many degrees and stateside licences you have, you need a Hawaii license to practice here. It's the same with teaching. You could have a Ph.D., but you still need a fifth-year diploma from UH to teach in the Hawaii public schools.

Jack Burns ran against Joseph Farrington for delegate to Congress in 1948 and got swamped. Now he runs against Farrington's widow, Elizabeth. His power base is the nisei vets from the 100th and 442nd and the ILWU. When Daniel Inouye announced he's running for a House seat, Danny Lowe said, "Hey, he got it made. If things get rough, all he gotta do is show them his missing arm."

Sure enough, when the Republican "Truth Squad" rush up the platform, grab the microphone and call the Democrats "tools of the ILWU and Communists," Inouye grabs back the microphone with his left arm and shouts, "I lost one arm fighting the Fascists, I'll give this other arm to fight the Communists!" The Truth Squad run off the platform with their tails between their legs.

We're glued to our radio on election night. Kaimuki goes 90 percent Democratic. Democrats win 2/3 of the territorial House and Senate, and nearly half of them are nisei! John Burns loses to Elizabeth Farrington by less than 1,000 votes out of 140,000! I thought we had a chance of winning but not this big! Yoshio Nishikawa, a friend from my boxing days, is a senator from Maui. Tommy Hida, another of my boxing fans, is supervisor in Maui County. *Nothing's gonna change,* I used to think. *Now things are exploding.*

Ames don't show up at the office for several days. "He's not feeling well," Grace Chun, the secretary, says.

Then Kiyo marries an Audrey Dutton from Minnesota,

and Audrey moves in with Kiyo and Ann. "You can be one-on-one with most haole girls. They're independent. . . ." he writes.

"You watch, Tsuneko's going to marry to a haole too!" I warn Mama when I invite them to Honolulu for the holidays.

"She's going with a boy from Guam," she says.

"Oh, yeah? What does Kiyo say?"

"He says whatever Tsuneko wants is fine with him. He says the boy is very nice. But I told her we didn't send her to college so that she could marry a boy from Guam."

"You're not sending her. Kiyo is."

"It's the same thing."

"I told you. The girls are not going to help you. They'll get married."

Then before the year ends Sadao Ono, whom we called *anshan,* or elder brother, dies of a stroke. The guy is so hard luck. After his mother, *Obaban,* died, he got into one accident after another. He got hit by a car while riding his motorcycle and was left for dead on the *pali* road. Another time he climbed a tree to pick mangoes for the kid next door and fell and nearly died. Both times he was drunk. Papa thought marriage would cure him and found him a wife from Paia. He came out to Honolulu to make a fresh start, but he couldn't stop drinking. He got demoted from finishing carpenter to running the electrical saws.

Papa comes to Kalihi for the funeral. It's real sad, dying at 49, leaving behind a wife and 5 kids. Chiaki, the eldest, cries and cries. At 15 he's now the head of the house.

Then I learn that Froggy, my pal from first grade, is killed on Front Street when the car he's driving rams the concrete abutment over the stream near the pineapple cannery. His knee gave way and he couldn't brake, people said. He quit the plantation and was making a good living in real estate. I put a $20 bill in an envelope and send it to his parents in Mill Camp.

19

Audrey

The Democratic sweep of '54 goes nowhere. Gov. King vetoes every bill the legislature passes. Unless Hawaii can become a state and elect its own governor, it's status quo. Truman recommended statehood in '48, as does Eisenhower now. The House of Reps passed the statehood bill several times, and each time the Senate voted it down. "How would you like a Senator Yamamoto to be sitting next to you?" a senator from the deep South said. Now they use communism as the excuse.

Bobo Olson defended his title a couple more times after Kid Gavilan. Then he floored and beat Joey Maxim, who'd beaten Sugar Ray Robinson in a light-heavyweight title fight. Actually, Sugar Ray got beat by the 110-degree heat. He vomited in the ring and gave up after the 13th round.

Mama talks Ann out of marrying the Guamanian, and she graduates Phi Beta Kappa and gets engaged to the youngest son of the prestigious Kono family. Brian's late father owned a store in Waipahu. His older sister is married to Doc Sawada, a top surgeon and the first nisei on the UH Board of Regents. Two brothers are lawyers, another a doctor, and Brian has a Ph.D. in anatomy.

"When I think of the Konos, even I bow my head," Papa tells Mama.

"He should bow his head to his sons!" I tell her.

In June Kiyo comes home with Audrey Dutton. She had worked at a Washington, D.C. public library. Kiyo asks if they can stay with us. I expect him to; we get lots of catching up to do. I take the afternoon off and pick them up at the airport.

"It's like walking into a oven. You know, all the time I was growing up in Pepelau, I kept thinking there had to be a cooler place," Kiyo says.

"Oh, this is nothing compared to a Minnesota summer. You could cut the humidity with a knife," Audrey says.

"You guys hungry? I'll take you to Pagoda. It's air conditioned."

Audrey is short, slightly overweight, and in her 30s. Her nose wells up at the end.

As soon as we sit down, Alky Dawson, who's on the boxing commission, comes over to our table. We talk about Bobo Olson and the great year he's having.

"Have you watched him on TV?" Audrey asks.

"Yeah, we get it here delayed," I say.

"Well, his hands are slow. He's fine as long as he fights people like Joey Maxim."

"What about Kid Gavilan?" Alky says.

"Gavilan is flashy, but he's powder puff," Audrey says.

"Like Gene Tunney?" Alky says, laughing.

"That was foot speed!" Audrey says, and we all laugh. "Olson would be in trouble with somebody with both punch and hand speed."

"Like who?" Alky asks.

"Ray Robinson, Archie Moore."

"How would you like to be a boxing judge? We're looking for somebody. You'd be the first woman judge in Hawaii."

Audrey turns red and turns to Kiyo.

"Naw, we're leaving for the states in a month," Kiyo says.

"You'd make a great judge," Alky says. "Too bad."

Audrey talks a mile a minute after Alky leaves. Some high school students came into her library looking for *Oranges and Peaches*. "D'you know what they wanted? *Origin of Species!*" She whoops with laughter. "Then there was this essay a student wrote. It ended up with, 'You cannot fool John Q. Pubic!' "

Audrey loves to talk. She was born in a ghost lumber town near the Canadian border, of seventh-generation Anglophobes. "What saves me is I'm one-sixteenth Chippewa," she says. Her grandparents hated each other. Her grandmother was carrying her lover's child when her family, who used to give her shoelaces for Christmas, forced her to marry Audrey's grandfather Dutton, who was 20 years older. Two more boys were born after the love child, Harry. Her grandmother naturally favored Harry. Then her grandfather's arteries hardened and he became a raving paranoid. Her parents had the same loveless marriage. Her father was nearly deaf and refused to wear a hearing aid or change out of his greasy mechanic's coveralls. Her mother was so starved for company she'd monopolize any friends Audrey brought home. What kept Audrey from going nuts were books.

"You must read encyclopedias," I say.

"That's the story of my life! People call me a walking encyclopedia! When I was biting my fingernails preparing for my summa orals, my advisor told the other professors, 'You don't have to worry about Miss Dutton, she can talk a leg off a horse, she's a walking encyclopedia.' Now they all say, 'You don't have to worry about Audrey, she can take care of herself.' The point is I *want* to be worried about. Mother used to tell me, 'You don't have to get married, you know. You can become a teacher. Many women do that and are quite happy.' Ugh! She must've thought I was a freak. Why else would I prefer to listen to the New York Philharmonic on Saturday afternoons? The truth was she wanted to listen to 'Fibber McGee' or something else. College saved me. Naturally, I had to work my way. . . ."

She's like a child. She holds nothing back. She graduated summa cum laude from Univ. of Minnesota in 3 years, scored 200 on her IQ test. It's not bragging if it's true. I like it when they put everything on the table, scars and all. Bulaheads hold back too much.

"I mistrust the strong, silent types. They make you do all the work while they sit back and act like they're deep in thought. Yes, 'it *is* wiser to remain silent and be thought dumb than speak and remove all doubt!' "

"That's right!" I say. You wouldn't notice the nose so much except she keeps fingering it.

She's a hit with the kids too. "How about a nightcap?" I offer when we come home from the Waikiki Tavern.

"Maybe a small one," Audrey says, head weaving. 11:00 P.M. is 2:00 A.M. their time.

"You know," Kiyo says, "Danny's and Marcia's English have really improved."

"Nahhh." I laugh. "They putting on a show for you and Audrey. As soon as you leave, they go back to pidgin."

"What grade you was? GS-11?" I ask Kiyo.

"Naw, GS-7."

"You get only a GS-7 even with college?"

"That's what I was too," Audrey slurs.

"The Armed Forces Security Agency came looking for translators at Columbia starting at GS-9. I didn't get cleared," Kiyo says.

"Same thing happened to me at the Library of Congress, of all places!" Audrey says.

"Why?"

"Who knows?" Audrey says.

"Maybe because I canvassed for Henry Wallace in the '48 election," Kiyo says.

"I campaigned for him too in upstate New York. The farmers kept asking, 'Why did he kill all the pigs?' " Audrey shrugs. "What could I say? It was the New Deal policy to raise the price of pork."

"You guys Communists?" I pour them more straight J&B and we keep lighting up.

"Nah." Kiyo laughs.

"Guilt by association is just as damning," Audrey says.

"I'm glad I didn't get accepted. Guys who work there act spooked. 'Let's have a drink,' I asked John Conway. We used to drink at the West End all the time. But this time he turned and looked around to make sure nobody was tailing him. Guys I knew at the military intelligence school work at the same place. They act the same way. They must be translating something super-secret like the bacteriological experiments the Japanese army conducted on the Chinese in Manchuria. The information was so important to the U.S. Army, they hushed it all up. Nobody was brought to trial, nobody was even charged," Kiyo says.

"Why are you surprised? All governments cover up. It's the nature of the beast," Audrey says.

"Well, some governments cover up more than others," Kiyo says.

"Of course, dictatorships. Everybody knows that."

"And group-oriented cultures," Kiyo says after a pause, sipping his J&B.

"Yes, all authoritarian systems!" Audrey lights up and slaps the matchbook on the coffee table, weaving.

"But the covering up need not come from the top."

"How so?"

"The group does it. It stifles dissent and encourages conformity and cover-up."

"You know, Morris, you should become a historian, not a playwright," Audrey says, weaving, spewing smoke.

"So you gonna study play writing at Yale?" I break in. "For an M.A.?"

"It's a Ph.T., 'putting hubby through,' " Audrey slurs.

"I still got over a year on my GI Bill."

"You'll never get produced," she mumbles.

"I don't expect to make money from it," Kiyo says.

"So why try it? Why not a Ph.T. in history?"

"I'm making a G a month now. That's about a GS-12," I say to change the subject.

"Good for you," Kiyo says as Audrey nods off.

He squashes her cigarette and wakes her, and guides her toward their bedroom.

"I love you, Morris," she mumbles, "but I have to show people I didn't marry you because I couldn't get a white man, d'you understand, Morris?"

I look away and take a sip. *"Morris." I have a hard time calling him that. It sounds strange, like calling Miwa "Aileen."*

"Do you love me, Morris?" she slurs.

"Yes."

"Honest?"

"Honest."

I look off. *Why she keeps reminding me of Mama?*

"She all right?" I ask when he comes back.

"Yeah. She can't hold too much."

We sip J&B and look away.

Suddenly I feel so heavy. Like all my insides are pulled down to my feet. "You know, I feel so tired. I been hustling for so long. I cannot stop. I gotta keep on busting my ass. Even then I keep falling behind. I see these young college kids getting way ahead. Sometimes I feel I cracking up. I get so mad, I yell at Carol and the kids. Damn old futts, they—"

"Why don't you take a vacation? Get off the rock. Go to the mainland."

"Who's gonna look after the kids?"

"Can you take three weeks off from work?"

"Yeah, I think so."

"We'll go back to Kahana for a week, and then we'll come back and baby-sit the kids for three weeks."

"You sure?"

"Yeah."

"What about Audrey?"

"I'll show her around Oahu."

We keep swigging one shot after another. I always liked the kid. Now we have something else in common. I trust drinkers. Maybe that's why I'm at odds and ends with Georgie. Alcohol gives him the hives.

"Listen, when you go back there, why don't you talk to the folks about going back to live in Japan when Papa retires. That's what the Konos did with their old man. They all chipped in every month. We can do the same. Papa'll be getting Social Security plus a pension."

"They won't go for it."

"But talk to them. They listen to you."

"Hawaii's home to them. Besides, they just got their citizenship papers."

"All that means is it's two more votes for the ILWU."

"All their network is here. They can't go live among strangers at their age. They've been pretty good parents."

"To you! Not to me!"

"Would you trade them for the Shiotsugu or Mitsui parents?"

"Shit, outside of Takemoto *sensei* everbody there is a hick!"

The Mitsui family in Kahana had 8 boys and no girls. The father used to beat up the mother while the boys just watched even after they grew up. But as soon as the father retired they bought him a one-way ticket to Japan and stranded him there. Then they took turns looking after their mother.

"But try talk to them."

"Naw, all their children are here," Kiyo says.

"What you mean? Only me and Miwa are here. All you guys ran away. Remember Minoru Shiotsugu, Hachiro's oldest brother? He used to be my truck driver. Papa and Mama used to praise him to my face. The guy's a braggart. He tried to bully me. Now he's telling his mother, 'You watch, Hachiro and Miwa will be the ones looking after the Oyama parents when they get old.' His mother told Mama, 'Don't you feel lonely, letting your children fly out of your hands?' Damn old futts, they're getting a free ride. They never had to look after *their* parents in their old age, but they expect us to look after them. Not only that, today the kids are demanding! We get it from both sides!"

"Why don't *you* talk to them?" he asks.

"They'll accuse me of trying to get rid of them."

We fly hours and hours over the ocean, leaving all the worries behind. The vibrations lull me to sleep. Even Carol falls asleep. Then we land in magical fog when we were sweltering 9 hours ago. Next day we rent a car and drive to the wine country. We stop at the lookout near the Golden Gate Bridge and watch the fog come tumbling over the ridge like giant balls of cotton candy. Carol says maybe we should call Georgie and Betty, who live in Pocomo 280 miles to the south. No, I say, this vacation is for us, not family. We eat at the best restaurants. People dress sloppy in Honolulu; there's litter everywhere. Frisco is brisk and clean; women wear hats and white gloves.

Then we fly another 8½ hours to New York. Miles and miles of mountains and rivers and forests and farmlands. Admiral Yamamoto was stationed in Washington, D.C., and knew the size of the U.S. His only hope was to cripple the U.S. fleet and then get a negotiated truce. How could he even think of a negotiated truce after the sneak attack on Pearl Harbor? Even if Japan had delivered the declaration of war on time, it would've been a sneak attack. Their planes were in position to strike. In boxing it'd be like standing over your seated opponent and hitting him as soon as the bell rings. It's samurai mentality—ambush is fair play.

Manhattan is like a 100-block county fair. Delicatessens are open all night. People mill about till dawn. There's so much energy in the air, you forget the heat. Every minute something is happening. Central Park, the Metropolitan Museum, Rockefeller Center, Broadway—they're all close by. Carol has trouble keeping up with me, her stockings falling down to her ankles. I feel like walking all the way to the Battery, but we take the subway for Carol's sake and visit the Statue of Liberty. There are great restaurants everywhere, uptown, in the Village. We eat and drink first class, spend and tip big. Every block is an eating adventure.

On the night of June 22nd we watch Bobo Olson fight Archie Moore live on the TV in our room at the Barbizon Plaza. It's for Moore's light-heavyweight crown. Back in Honolulu I'd have to go the the Columbia Bar to watch the replay a couple days later. Naturally, I'm all for the local boy. But right off the bat I feel uneasy. Bobo looks so small beside Moore. Moore toys with Bobo. He pushes him off, clinches, and ties him up whenever he wants. Bobo is slow while Moore's hands are quick. Bobo's only hope is to wear down Archie; he's 26 to Archie's 38. They feel each other out for 2 rounds. Then it happens in a flash. Moore lands a right to Bobo's chin. It's so fast you don't even see it, but Bobo's out cold. After the referee raises his hand, Moore is nonchalantly combing his hair in the middle of the ring. *Boy, why did I think he had a chance?*

Flying home, we're in the air for almost 17 hours straight. Now I'm so anxious to get home the planes feel like they're crawling. *How are the kids? Hope they weren't too much for Audrey and Kiyo.* I feel tired but rested when we land.

I treat everybody to a Chinese dinner in Moiliili.
"I usually improve when I do the same thing over and over, but I kept poking myself with the safety pin everytime I changed Gerald's diaper," Audrey says. "But what really surprised me was when I first turned him around. 'My God, there's the Mongol spot!' I told Morris. D'you know what he said? 'I thought everybody had it.'"
"It disappears after a year," Carol says.
"I've read about it but never seen one."
Danny, Marcia, and Chrys loved Audrey's cooking, but Uncle Kiyo fed them only hot dogs.
"You know why?" Kiyo says. "I made them meatballs and spaghetti with this terrific sauce. They wouldn't touch it. So I said, 'Okay, hot dogs!'"
They all liked hot dogs except Audrey.
Afterward I hand Kiyo $300.
"Wha-for?"
"Baby-sitting. It's worth hundred a week."
"I don't need it. I don't have any pressure. I got no kids."
"You will later."
"Naw, I'm not having kids."
"What Audrey say?"
"She agrees."
"You wasting lots of IQs." I put the money in his pocket.

Couple days later, Kiyo and Audrey fly to the mainland without stopping by. I take the whole family to Honolulu Airport to see them off. We have coffee and ice cream while they wait for their plane. I worry about them. *How long Kiyo expects a haole wife gonna stick with a starving playwright? Not even a nisei wife would put up with it for long.*

In September Chrys starts kindergarten at Washington School only a block away. Carol has only Gerald at home now and she opens a small dress shop in Kapahulu. We also rent the housekeeping unit in the back of the house to a widow and her child.

In November a Democrat, John A. Burns, is elected delegate to Congress for the first time in Hawaiian history.

Then Senator James Eastland of Mississippi schedules another Communist hearing in Honolulu. At a testimonial dinner for Jack Hall, Harry Bridges threatens to shut down most of Hawaii as a protest. Sure enough, when the hearing opens on November 30, about 3,000 of 24,000 ILWU workers walk off their jobs. All the union people take the Fifth, and both Gov. King and ex-Gov. Stainback accuse the ILWU of being Communist. It's comical since Edward S. Sylva, a long-standing anti-Communist, was fired by Gov. King for attending the Jack Hall testimonial dinner. Sylva complained that the ILWU was now a legitimate force and communism a minor problem here. Newly elected John Burns said the ILWU was now respectable. The Eastland Committee came out with their tired old findings: the ILWU and United Public Workers were tools of the Soviet Union. But we're still waiting to see if they send Jack Hall to jail and bust the union.

Sugar Ray Robinson makes a comeback and fights Bobo for the middleweight crown in Chicago. Sugar Ray is 35 and Bobo 27. Eight years ago Sugar Ray KO'd Bobo in the thirteenth round. Now Sugar Ray KO's him in the second. I had $20 on Bobo.

20

Barbara Hutton

In March Barbara Hutton checks in at the Royal Hawaiian with her entourage. Chuck pays the hotel $15,000 to close the bar and lanai from 1:00 to 4:00 P.M. and invites his *mahu* and society friends to her party. She's thinking of building a house in Mexico for her new husband, the German tennis champion. He was refused a visa to the U.S. because he is a *mahu*. So they wintered in Cuernavaca, where she bought 30 acres from a Mexican contractor.

"She wants to build a Japanese-style mansion to house her collection of Oriental antiques. That's what millionaires do. They collect, then they build a house for their collections," Chuck explains.

Couple years back Doris Duke asked Chuck how much it would cost to gold-leaf a Moorish onion dome. She collected Persian antiques at Shangri-la, her Diamond Head estate. Chuck asked me to check out the cost of gold-leafing. I phoned Builders Gold. My pidgin accent must've turned him off. "No, you'd better forget it. It'll cost too much," the haole said, laughing. "Oh, okay . . ." I said, wondering who else I could call. "Who's your client?" he asked just before hanging up. "Doris Duke." "I'll be right over!" In the end Doris Duke decided not to build.

Chuck practically lives at the Royal Hawaiian the next few days, sketching and developing designs for Barbara Hutton's *sumiya*, or "house at the corner." I do the elevations for the floor plans. What a program! Start with a detached guest house, a lanai and bar, a swimming pool, a tennis court, then an open entrance lanai to the sliding glass panels of the living room. A wooden bridge in an enclosed open court is to be the only access to the bedroom suite, which is to have tatami floors but a bed and dressing counter. The dining room is to be for floor-sitting with a well under the table for the diners' legs; the living room is all Western with wall-to-wall carpets. The spread-out plan includes a 40-seat Kabuki-style theatre.

A purely Japanese house doesn't need an architect. It builds itself up from the 3′ × 6′ tatami module. The number of tatamis used determines the spacing of the posts and height of the ceiling. The Japanese-style houses we did in Hawaii were *hapa*. The pitched roof and overhanging eaves suited our winter rains. We didn't have to contend with the Japanese winter so we used sliding glass panels between the posts, which brought in the outdoors. They were furnished with tables, chairs, and beds. Floor-based living and multipurpose rooms are for making maximum use of limited space.

"You have to *spend* money to make money," Chuck says, all smiles. Barbara Hutton pays him a $10,000 retainer to build a $1,000,000 *sumiya*.

"She's leaving for San Francisco at the end of the month and then to Italy and France. We have to sign her before she changes her mind. It's a difference between ten thousand and one hundred thousand dollars."

"I cannot do it just with Ted. I need extra help."

He agrees to hire 2 temporary draftsmen.

"You can save thirty days if you pick a contractor now. I don't know how much materials and labor cost in Japan, but at three hundred sixty yen to a dollar, shouldn't be much. I bet you can get quality without asking for low bids," I say.

"I'm checking on references now."

The next day Chuck brings a set of photos and affidavits of her antique collection.

"It shouldn't be difficult," he says. "The collection isn't even one percent of Winterthur's. But the house has to be more than a mere envelope. It has to be authentic and conform to the periods of the pieces."

I examine the 6- and 8-panel screens, an antique door painted with peacock and chrysanthemum, ink-brush drawings, paintings, lacquer boxes, trays, etc.

"I cannot do it just by books. I have to go to Japan to look at the real stuff."

"I'll send you when I get the builder picked. Barbara has an exhibit of Chinese porcelain at the Academy of Arts. You should look at them too."

I have Ted break in Tom Chang and Sam Inoki, the temporary helps. Then I pile their "In" baskets with my prelims.

"You gotta convert everything to metric. Japan and Mexico are metric. No worry about the lettering and dimensioning. As long as they legible. Do the lettering and dimensioning lines free-hand . . . like this. Nemmind if a little crooked or one-sixteenth inch off. This rush job. *Ukupau*."

Luckily we don't have the time-consuming details of windows and doors. Chuck flies to Cuernavaca to examine the site with a Mexican civil engineer. He checks the zoning laws and picks a project manager. I consult the engineers here. Electricians and plumbers will be Mexican.

I cram and cram. The *sumiya* came into being in the late 1600s with the rise of the merchant class. Without wars the samurai fell into poverty. Money, not rice, became the medium of exchange, and rich merchants built hideaway *sumiya*s for their mistresses. Barbara Hutton's "house at the corner" will be that in name only. It's too small. She'll need the bigger *shoin/sukiya*, which conforms to the period of her antiques. The *sukiya* is a later version of the formal *shoin*. It's less religious and more rustic and richly detailed, though the skeleton is the same—tightly joined Japanese cypress posts and beams, floor posts on small foundation stones, floor 2 feet off the ground.

Chuck stops by every day and stands over us. "We're talking ninety thousand dollars! Time is worth ninety thousand! She's leaving for Paris in a month and half!"

"How about helping us?"

"The first job of the architect is to bring in the job. I've done that. Your job is to do the drawings."

"Some offices, the bosses work on the board with the draftsmen," I say.

"Yes, I know. The ones that don't have enough to do."

He's good at schematics and design development, and he makes good presentation drawings and renderings, but he's sloppy in the details, knowing I'd fill them in.

I draw so hard and fast I see lines when I close my eyes. I stand at the board for hours, then come back after supper. I read in bed and wake up in the middle of the night, remembering one more detail. I work 16 hours, sleep 5 hours. I rush so hard food sits in a lump in my stomach.

"You have to slow down," Carol says. "Go get *shiatsu*."

I'm glad she leaves me alone at times like this. *A haole wife would demand her daily quota of attention.*

Then one night Carol says at supper, "You have to talk to Chrys."

"Cannot wait? I'm so busy."

"No," she says.

She won't bother me unless it's real important. She knows my work comes first. *I'm still struggling.*

Chrys vomited in Miss Kishi's first-grade class. It was parents' day, and when Carol and the other parents got to her class, Chrys burst into tears.

"Why you a crybaby, Chrys? You scared of Miss Kishi?" I hold her in my lap.

"You know what Miss Kishi told her afterward? 'You didn't have to do that in front of everybody,' " Carol says.

"How come you wen cry?" She hides her face in my shoulder.

"How come you wen vomit? You sick?" I say.

"You shouldn't speak pidgin. It's a bad example," Carol says.

"How come you vomited, Chrys? Why did you cry?"

"I hide the peas." She sniffs.

"Where?"

"Under the plate."

"So you don't like peas?"

She shakes her head.

"So why you vomit?"

"Miss Kishi wen make me eat the peas."

"Thass why you vomited?"

She nods and hides her face.

"But why did you cry today?" Carol asks.

She curls around me again. "I bet I know why," I say. "You want to show Miss Kishi up, yeah? You want to show she one mean witch, yeah?"

Quick nods.

"Phew! I thought maybe she was r-e-t-a-r-d-e-d," I tell Carol. It's the first thing the Kahana wahines bring up. Masaru Nakai worked for the Army in Japan and married a Japan girl. When he came back last year, the women said, "Oh, you know Masaru Nakai is back. His daughter is retarded . . ."

"She shouldn't be teaching first grade. She's such a disciplinarian. She treats them like they were fourth or fifth graders," Carol says.

"She's a Pepelau girl too."

"Yeah, she was two grades behind me," Carol says.

I take a night off. I drop by the Columbia Bar.

"Hey, I hear your society architect wen catch one beeg fish, eh?"

"Yeah, I busting my ass. He wants it finished before she change her mind. It's a difference between hundred Gs and ten Gs."

"So he giving you one bonus?"

"He better."

"Eh, you know what your *mahu* boss wen tell my boss?" Dike Masuo says. He works for a haole architect too.

"Yeah, what?"

"He says Orientals shouldn't get paid so much because they save half of what they make."

"Oh, yeah?"

"Yeah."

"Well, he going give me a big bonus. I saving him ninety Gs. Hey, you guys know what's a 'bidet'?"

"What that?" Dike says.

"Nobody know? Where's Lenny? He'd know. It's a washbasin sunk in the bathroom floor. The French wahines, they squat over it to wash their twats."

For the first time in 2 weeks I get a good night's sleep.

After couple of weeks, Chuck gets the name of a reputable contractor in Kyoto.

"He has his own crew of carpenters, plasterers, and roofers. No subcontractors. I have it from an unimpeachable source his craftsmanship is museum quality," he says.

"Great!" I say. We'll be saving 3–4 weeks, the time it takes for the contractors to send in their bids.

Now my specs can read "top-quality *hinoki* lumber; construction methods of the seventeenth century; all joinery, no nails except when unavoidable and they must be invisible; walls of earthen plaster . . ."

Chuck makes blueprints of each working drawing and specs and mails them to Mr. Harada, the contractor. The budget is the least of our worries. Time is worth 90 Gs.

We finish the drawings, but Barbara Hutton has left for Frisco and time is running out.

"I'll give you a twenty-five dollars per diem. You people can live on half of what it takes us," Chuck says.

"Bullshit! I got haole taste!"

"All right, bring back all your bills."

I ask Ted Noguchi, a Pepelau boy and travel agent, to reserve me rooms in cheap hotels in Tokyo and Kyoto. "I'll get you Japanese-style *ryokan*s," he says. "They're half the price of swanky hotels."

"You going to Tokyo? Go see Mrs. Kanai," Masayuki Shiroma, my barber, says. "She one widow now." The Shiromas had a barbershop on Main Street in Pepelau before the war, and they were pillars of the Methodist Church. The Kanais left for Japan in 1939, and Rev. Kanai died during the war.

It must've been the 4 J&B's and the vibration of the plane —I sleep zonked out and wake up next morning in Tokyo. It's a sprawling shantytown, teeming with Japanese. I check in and take a cab. The driver is a white-gloved kamikaze, swerving into alleys at full speed, dodging oncoming cars at the last second. It's a maze of alleys and streets. Houses sprang up haphazardly after the firebombs demolished the city. He finally arrives at the address. *"Hai,"* he says. It's a slum.

"Kanai-san! Kanai-san!" I call into the 2-story woodframe house.

An old woman in a faded print dress comes out and peers up at me through rimless glasses. Her hair, in a bun, is snow-white. The *okusan* I knew stood straight, a foot taller than her husband, the reverend. Unlike him, she spoke perfect English, and she dressed in the latest flapper hats and flowing silk gowns.

"*Okusan*, how are you? *Hisashi buri ne?* Do you remember me? I am Oyama Toshio. I was the bad boy Kanai *sensei* kicked out of Japanese language school." I crouch to show myself. *She must be only in her 50s!*

"Ah, Oyama Toshio. You weren't bad. You just had lots of energy," she says in English.

"I'm sorry to hear about Reverend Kanai," I say. I remember his hitting me in class when I told him I was quitting.

"It was merciful in a way," she says. "He suffered during

the war. He kept telling people Japan can't win. They don't realize how vast America is, and its people are not spoiled and divided but individuals in a democracy, and they'd rise up in a body after an attack like Pearl Harbor and never settle for a negotiated truce. He refused to take part in the air-raid drills, and neighbors came to our house at night to throw stones."

"Why did you come back here?"

"Reverend Kanai and I were childless. We wanted to be among kin. 'It's *zannen* to die in a strange land,' I used to say. It seemed so important then. Also we thought we could do some good here with our knowledge of America and our command of English. All through the war we were forbidden to speak English. During the early years, they'd broadcast baseball games. The announcers were forbidden to say 'hitto' for 'hit.' The government had them say, *anda,* 'safe hit.' "

"Let's have lunch," I say.

"Do you realize you have a cousin living nearby?" she says when we sit down at a noodle shop. "She works at a toy factory across town. Did you know your late aunt, Chiyako? Yoshiko is her child from her first marriage. Chiyako divorced her first husband and remarried Takashi Kuni, the older brother of Mr. Kuni of Kahana. She had two children by him, then she died soon after the war ended. Mr. Kuni remarried and has two more children."

She's full of questions about Pepelau and the people in the congregation.

"The church is still there. I remember your tenth-grade class put on a Shakespeare play in Japanese for their graduation."

"Yes. *Hamlet.* Those were happy days."

I put ten 10,000 yen notes into her hand when I leave.

"No, no, no," she says, and pushes my hand away.

I fold the money and push it down her neckline.

"No, no!" she says, backing off, "people will talk."

It's only two hundred seventy-eight dollars American.

She's bowing and bowing when I look back. It shakes me up. *How can people change so much? She used to be so proud. Everybody called her "Okusan." She gave Mrs. Woods hell when Kiyo was hit by the car in front of the church. Now she's cowed by what people will say.*

I call on the Kunis after supper. He looks like his brother, Robert, who's now the principal of Kahana Grade School. The same round face and round *mempachi* eyes. Everybody looked up to Robert Kuni. He was the first success from Kahana.

I could've recognized Yoshiko anywhere. She walks like sister Ann—back straight, ass out. I make small talk with Mr. Kuni and his wife while I watch Yoshiko wash the dishes, bathe her 2 step-sisters and put them to bed. The older boy and girl are Chiyako's so they're Yoshiko's half-siblings. Finally Yoshiko is free and comes to sit with us on the tatami. I'm mad as hell! I came to see her, not them!

"How are you?"

"*Kekko.* How is your mother?" she asks.

"Fine."

We keep on making small talk, waiting for her step-parents to leave. But they sit there for the next 2 hours.

"Well, I better be going." I get up madder than hell. Damn Japs! They always take advantage!

"Thank you for all the gifts. Please give my regards to your mother and father," Yoshiko says, and follows me into the alley.

"You realize, they're making a *baka* of you!? Leave! You owe them nothing! You're not even the same blood! If you're not married the next time I come, I'm taking you to Hawaii! I'll find you a husband there!" *Even Kazuo Kawai would be an improvement.*

"*Hai,*" she says, bowing. Then she says, "Please forgive my mother *ne?*"

"*Nani?*"

"All she talked about before she died was how badly she treated your mother."

"What are you talking about?"

"Mother was ten when your mother arrived in Hawaii. She treated your mother very badly. 'I should've apologized, I should've apologized,' she kept saying when she was dying. Please forgive her, *ne?*"

"That's ancient history. It's forgotten," I say. "But I'm warning you." I shake my finger. "They have no conscience. They'll treat you like a maid forever. *You* have to leave. If you're not married and out of here the next time I come—"

"Oh," Mr. Kuni says as he steps out, "I was worried when you didn't come back."

"*Sayonara.*" Yoshiko bows.

"Remember what I said," I say.

"What did he say?" I hear the parasite asking her as I leave, and I get even madder.

The next day I go to a swank hotel and "buy" a postdated receipt for the night, then get receipts from an expensive restaurant, and fly to Kyoto. Jiro Harada and his men meet me at the airport. One carries the prints, another a folder with the photos, a third with a fat valise. Harada is about my age, tall for a Japanese, 5'8".

"*Sensei.*" He bows and his men bow with him. *Nobody ever called me* "sensei"!

"Where dzu you wanz go firsto?" Harada asks.

"Take me to my *ryokan,* then I want to see some of the works you did."

We pile into his '56 Chevy coupe. It's the biggest car on the road. Kyoto was spared bombing during the war. American intelligence said there was nothing strategic there. It's serene compared to bustling Tokyo.

At the *ryokan* I dig out my prints and give Harada copies of the last quarter of the prints.

Then we drive to a *sukiya* he restored. Inside and out, the materials and crafstmanship are first-rate. A "floating" Japanese ceiling and *hinoki* framing. *Great!*

"Just like your *sukiya,*" I compliment him.

"No, no, mine outside onry" Harada says.

"Did you study the photos?" I ask.

"*Hai, hai.*" He nods several times.

I say in slow English, "I need *ramma* and *fusuma* and other details that are of the periods of the antiques. For instance, the living room is all Western. Wall-to-wall carpets, Chinese rosewood coffee table and chairs, sofas and ottomans. *Wakaru?*"

He nods quickly. "Yes, yes."

"All the screens will be in both the dining and living rooms."

"One screen early Tokugawa, 1630 to 1730, other ones late Tokugawa, 1730 to 1880, Kano school," he says.

We drive all over Kyoto. He shows me more works he's

done and the interior details for early and late Tokugawa. We sketch and photograph. It's not so much the periods and ideas I want to nail down, but the visual—how will they look beside the panel of ink-brush paintings. For instance, Hutton's little lacquer boxes are of Momoyama period, and would fit best somewhere in the bedroom suite. So I'll be dealing at most with 3 periods.

They offer to treat me to supper, but I say no, let's go to the compound and order take-outs and work on my latest prints and the interior details. It's past midnight when they drive me to my *ryokan.*

We spend another 15-hour day, now all at the compound. I push them like I pushed Ted and my 2 helpers. I keep selecting, discarding, selecting the right details to conform not only to the periods but also to the style of the pieces—the peacock and chrysanthemum door leading to the living room or to the screens in the vestibule. And I push them to work their abacuses to come up with estimates.

Finally, at dusk on the third day Harada comes up with an estimate—325,000,000 yen. "It can't go any higher," he says.

"Did you include ocean freight of the materials?"

"Yes."

"What about transportation of your men? And their room and board while there. The exchange will be in pesos. I don't know if you'll gain or lose with the yen. You're not including the wall and the main gate and stone lantern?"

"No, just insai house."

"You'll probably need the ten percent cushion. No telling how much the Mexican *yakunin* will ask. Sign it for three-sixty. There's bound to be hidden expenses. The steamship cost will be in yen? The yen is nothing if you have to pay in dollars."

"*Hai, hai, okage sama de,*" he says, bowing deeply, and all his men bow. I like the guy. He's like Bob Agena, a general contractor I use back home. I don't have to explain every omission and detail. He can follow my thoughts. He has a shock of black, greasy hair. He keeps his arms to his sides, feet together. They all have that stiffness, like they're ready to bow or click their heels. They could be niseis except for the stiffness and baggy pants. Hawaii is wide open compared to their packed-like-sardines space.

"We take you now to *sumiya* for geisha party," he says. "Onry *sumiya* in oru Jappan."

I ask them to drive me to the swankiest hotel and restaurant.

"*Chotto matte,*" I say, and run in to "buy" receipts for my $50 per diem.

The *sumiya* is barely big enough for our party of 20. They must've reserved it months ago. I laugh. *Chuck would have a fit if we built a real "sumiya." It'd cost only 100 Gs at the most.*

We have *shabu-shabu*—a meat stew that don't exist in Hawaii. The geishas pour the *sake*. Harada and his men toast me one after the other and I toast them back, as is the custom.

I wag a finger at Harada. "You *sensei*. Me, *deshi*," I say, tapping my chest.

"No-no-no," he says, palm fluttering. You *sensei*. Me *deshi*."

"What you think Barbara Hutton house? Outside *sukiya*, inside all mix up?"

"Insai all mixu uppu orai," Harada says.

Pretty soon we're singing and clapping. I have a nice buzz and remember the Columbia back home. *Niseis too need booze to loosen up, but these guys get drunk faster and act real tipsy and silly.*

"*Sensei, kampai.*" They keep toasting.

The next morning Harada and his men drive me to the airport on a flight to Tokyo. I look forward to flying to Honolulu. It'll give me a chance to sleep.

When I get back, I show Chuck the receipts I "bought" in Tokyo and Kyoto and get my $50 per diem.

Chuck flies to San Francisco to see Barbara Hutton. He's gone for a week and comes back gliding into the office. All the *mahu* gestures come out, the prancing, the wrist action. He's collecting the 100 Gs in 3 installments to save on taxes and he's leaving on a 4-month cruise around the world.

"You're not giving us a bonus!?" I ask.

"I pay you more than any draftsman makes," he says.

"Yeah, but this was extra! I bust my ass! I push my boys!"

"Check the other offices. Nobody gets one thousand a month."

"Yeah, but this was overtime! I put in sixteen hours a day! We finish in three months what takes eight months!"

Just then a *hapa* shoe-shine boy pokes his head in the doorway. "Shine? Shine?"

"Yes, give these boys a shine," Ames says.

I laugh. "Yeah, we'd better take the shine. That's all the bonus we going get!"

But afterward I stew. I yell at Carol and the kids and go out and get stinking drunk.

The next day Ames phones the office and asks me to bring his valise from the office and drive him to the airport. He's flying to Los Angeles to catch his boat.

I have a throbbing headache as I drive up Tantalus in the blinding sun and look for the address. Metal numbers soldered on grillwork gate. A pastel '57 Lincoln with fat tail fins and another fat-fender car crowd the driveway. It's a large, open-style Spanish colonial, stucco walls, red tile roof. The view sweeps from Diamond Head to Ewa. The blue ocean rises to the horizon. It's breezy and fragrant with plumerias. Ames came slumming to Kaimuki a month ago to get one of the books on Japanese architecture. He stepped into our kitchen and said, "Where d'you get this!? It's mine! It's an antique!" "You mean this rug!? It was mixed up with the laundry at the office. I thought it was a rag," I said. "It's worth a fortune!" he said. Luckily the washing machine had not hurt it.

"Oh, Chuck, your boy is here!" a young, skinny haole shrieks. "Can I get you a drink?"

"No thanks."

Couple more young men come out. Mainland haoles not yet tanned.

"So he's the tiger of Malaya," one of them says.

"He doesn't look ferocious, he's more—"

"Like a trade number!" they shriek, kicking up knees.

I'm boiling.

Ames has leis up to his ears.

"You ready?" I snarl.

The boys follow with the suitcases.

I get madder and madder as I drive down the mountain. When I reach the bottom, I let go. "You and your goddamn *mahu*s! You all the same! You think we nothing but houseboys! I going show you some day! I going get my license and I'll show you who needs who more! No draftsman in town working harder! Shit! I work around the clock for three months! I ignore my family! I push myself so hard I almost crack up and all I get is one shoe shine! Without me you nothing! You one parasite! Just like the plantation bosses! One more thing! You go around telling everybody Orientals overpaid, they save half of their pay!" I shake my finger. "You know, I can make you or break you! . . ." I yell and yell. He cringes against the door. I'm only 5'5" but I'm ready to hit this 6-foot slob!

I'm yelled out by the time we get to the airport. I help him with his suitcases.

"Have a good trip." I extend a hand, looking away.

It's a fingers-only limp handshake. *Why I offering this stupid handshake!?*

I drive back aimlessly. *What if he fire me? Shit, if he fire me, he fire me. Nobody indispensable. I sick of catching all the shit. I oughta blow up more often.*

III

1958-1964

21

Testing the Waters

"How's my boy?" Chuck puts his arm on my shoulder when he gets back.

"Fine, Chuck. And you?"

"Can't be better. Here's something for you."

It's a ring box and inside is a shiny, fat gold ring with a big aquamarine jade.

"Chee, thanks, Chuck."

"And this is from Barbara Hutton."

A smaller box holds a sparkling diamond.

"Will you thank her for me?" I feel real silly, having blown up 4 months ago.

I have it set right away. The jeweler says the jade ring is worth $700, the diamond $500.

One nice thing with Chuck, he don't hold grudges. He sends me on a site visit to Cuernavaca. I pay for Carol's plane fare and take her with me. We fly into L.A., then Mexico City, where Alfredo Ochoa, the project manager, meets us at the airport.

"Mr. Oyama?" He extends a hand. "I'm Alfredo."

"Call me Steve, Alfredo," I say. "This is my wife, Carol."

He's a good-looking guy in his 40s. We drive from Mexico City down to Cuernavaca. "It's the home of the international set. It's cooler than Honolulu," Chuck said. "It's five thousand feet." Mt. Popocatepetl looms like Mt. Fuji across the great valley.

Workers are everywhere, Mexican and Japanese.

"Ah, *sensei*." Harada bows.

The skeleton has already been reassembled and is waiting for the plumbers and electricians. It's always exciting to see your plans go up. *Is it as you visualized it?* I'm glad there wasn't much grading. A building should use the natural contour of the land and the surrounding vegetation.

I go over the prints with Harada. Materials and workers are everywhere. Mexican stonemasons are cutting stones for the wall that will rise from the valley floor to the terrace of the bedroom suite. It'll look like the stonewall foundations of Japanese castles. I step inside the living room and imagine looking out of the large glass panel to the terrace of the bedroom suite. The narrow bridgeway leads to the bedroom suite. I step out to the terrace. Snow-capped Mt. Popocatepetl across the valley looks unreal. *Chuck made good use of the views.* But the compound sprawls. "An architect is a whore; his first job is to please the client," I remember Lenny saying. *But my end of the program—a museum-quality building to house the antiques—should hold up.*

Ochoa is delighted when I quit. He's a gourmet and a drinker like me. He takes us to a fancy restaurant in Cuernavaca. We eat and drink past supper, then make the rounds of nightclubs and get to bed past 3.

I get a balloon-size hangover the next morning when he drives us back to Mexico City.

I rent a car at LAX and we drive north to see Georgie and Betty and their families in Pocomo. It was 7 years ago that Georgie got $50 from Johns Mansville for recruiting Yukio. Yukio went first and helped Georgie and Gertrude build their house while working swing or graveyard. Then Betty, Yukio, and their 3 kids lived with Georgie and Gertrude while they all worked on Yukio's and Betty's house. Afterward Georgie kept buying more lots on the block and building rental property. He'd lived in each new house for a few months so that he could keep building without a contractor's license. Then he quit college and Johns Mansville and worked as a draftsman out of his house.

"It's not functional," I say when he shows me his house.

"What do you mean?"

"Your dining room is too far from the kitchen."

"Trudy uses a food cart."

"That's what I mean."

"But I bought the design."

"I give you credit, though." The guy always hated school, but he had lots of push and he was people smart.

"You get enough work?"

"Oh, yeah, I get so busy, I farm some of the drafting to Yukio and Kristin."

"What's your fee?"

"Two to three percent."

"I get angry. He spends so much time in his office. Why doesn't he sleep there too?" Gertrude says.

"Us Oyamas, we've got two strikes against us. So everybody has to pitch in," I say.

Georgie is a natural artist. He won all kinds of prizes in language school for his drawings. His renderings look so effortless, but their proportions are off.

"They look top-heavy. You have to draw to scale."

"I knock them off in no time. All I'm interested in is the money," he says.

"Me too. But you have to get the proportions right. Every building you put up is your advertisement."

"At two percent they don't care."

Pocomo is a small farming town with one registered architect who farms out $20,000 jobs to Georgie. It must be because California is so big. In Hawaii the draftsmen who do side jobs of over 20 Gs get warnings from the jealous two-bit architects.

Driving back, I tell Carol, "It's a good thing we stayed in Hawaii. Mainland is haole land. Georgie has to brownnose the haoles for a living."

When we get back, the plantations are on strike again. A month earlier, in January, the Court of Appeals in San Francisco overturned the conviction of Jack Hall and the others. Communism is a dead issue. But now Hall and Goldblatt claim the Big 5 are using the profit from sugar to prop up their shipping, retail, and hotel ventures, and they ask for a 25-cent raise across the board. The Big 5 offer a 4-cent raise. The base pay is $1.12 an hour. The union had 25,000 workers in '46. Now it's down to 13,700. Frontier Mill has had a new manager since 1953, when Carlyle was fired. Now Carlyle acts as mediator for the union. Soon after he was fired, he drove through Kahana, and the guys drinking beer at the park yelled at him to come join them, and they all got drunk together. Swipe told him, "You used to be one mean buggah, you know." "Yeah, you wen kick out our family just because they wen intern my father," Congo said. "It was plantation policy. You couldn't live in the camp if nobody worked on the plantation," Carlyle said. AmFac fired him, he said, because he'd spent too much money clearing the rocks from the Launiupoko and Olowalu fields.

In April I go on a site visit to Hana for six cabins we designed for the Hana Hotel. I stop over in Kahana. Papa is chief cook of the Kahana soup kitchen, which feeds 400 people twice a day from both Kahana and Honokawai. He looks beat.

"How come you guys make my old man work so hard!?" I ask Bill Toda, the Kahana union rep.

"He volunteered. I told him we got lots of younger guys, but he says he wants to do it," Bill says.

"*Inaka no taiko-mochi*—a country bumpkin!" I yell at Mama. "He volunteers for all the jobs nobody else wants so he can act the big shot!"

"I guess he wants to show Jun he's as young as the nisei parents," she says. Scott Jun is now 14, the same as Danny Kenji.

The strike ends on June 6 after 128 days. The union gets 16 cents across the board plus 7 cents later. Both sides claim victory. Papa still looks beat when I visit a couple weeks later.

"Are you all right?"

He laughs and nods.

A noncollege draftsman needs 12 years of experience to take the exam for an architect's license. College grads need only 3.

My "friends" at the Columbia say, "Hey, they never wen pass one noncollege man in over ten years." "You bucking one stone wall."

"Yeah? So I'll be the first."

I feel real loose. The first time is just to test the waters.

The site planning problem is for a golf course. I design it with all 18 holes going in the same direction.

"I never knew they get a front nine and back nine! I gotta learn to golf!" I tell my drinking buddies.

"You don't golf, you *play* golf," Dick Kawasaki says.

"Is that right?" I ask Lenny.

We're the 3 biggest drinkers and Lenny is the biggest.

"Either one is correct. You heard of 'common usage'? Whatever is popular is acceptable. Just like 'Buddhahead' is more common than your 'Bulahead.' "

"You mean you keep accepting the mistake?" I ask.

"That's why we say 'normalcy' instead of 'normality,' 'Japan' instead of 'Nippon.' "

"What you mean, 'Japan instead of Nippon'?"

"The Chinese characters pronounced 'nippon' in Japanese is pronounced 'rih-pun' in Chinese. In transliteration the guttural

Chinese 'r' is spelled with a 'j.' The Europeans mispronounced it as 'j.' So Marco Polo said 'Chipangu' and the Portuguese said 'Japao.' It's a historic misnomer, like calling Native Americans 'Indians.' "

"Next time somebody calls me a Jap I'll tell um, 'It's a misnomer!' What's a misnomer?"

Lenny is tall and good-looking. Several guys with height and looks marry mainland haoles. They figure it's a shortcut out of the plantation, but most of them shortchange themselves in looks, education, or brains. In Lenny's case Greta is the one short-changed. She's real pretty, has a Ph.D. in linguistics from Univ. of Wisconsin, teaches at UH, and practically supports Lenny and their 2 girls. Landscape architects are starving even more than architects.

In December I get my test results. I pass the 12-hour section on design but flunk the rest. But design is 1/3 of the whole exam and is the toughest section. Several guys with only design left keep flunking it.

There are 11 of us in our "class of '58." Nobody passes all 7 sections, but Masato Nakamura, a Univ. of Washington grad, passes everything but site.

22

Statehood

In January Chuck goes to Cuernavaca with his friends for the housewarming of Barbara Hutton's *sumiya*. She separated from von Cramm (the tennis champ) some time ago and is now running around with a young Jimmy Douglas. Chuck returns with a commission to do a Japanese-style house for the caretaker. Also, Barbara Hutton wants authentic Japanese peasant clothes for her Mexican yardmen. But it's not a rush job and there are other jobs in the pipeline.

I take Carol with me this time, paying for her fare. We go to Kyoto in late April and are feted again by Jiro Harada and his men. The style of the caretaker's house has to conform with the *sumiya*. Harada sucks his breath when I show him the prints. It would cost 80 Gs in Honolulu.

The next stop on our itinerary is Hakata, where I'm to see samples of eighteenth-century peasant clothes. When we get to our hotel in Hakata, I'm greeted in the lobby by 12 of Papa's and Mama's relatives! *Damn! I shouldn't have bragged to the old farts!* It's uncanny—Aunt Aya, the baby who was left in Japan, looks like Papa with a wig, Aunt Masako has Miwa's wide cheeks, and Cousin Yasuo looks thin and constipated like Kiyo.

"I used to baby-sit you, Toshi-chan," Masako says, and holds me, giggling.

Mama actually looks soft compared to her sister Tomi.

I invite them to dinner and order filet mignon, and they all order filet mignon. The bill comes to 288,000 yen, or $800 American! Papa must've bragged I was doing Barbara Hutton's house. Yoshiko in Tokyo said grandfather (the thief) used to brag I was a boxing champion. *Damn Papa, he cannot compliment me once but he go bragging behind my back.*

"You know, Father is a failure! He came to Hawaii as a plantation worker and he's still a plantation worker! He'll die not having advanced himself one inch. Grandfather was worse! He took advantage of Father and Mother and left us $6,000 in debt!

Father couldn't even support his own family. I had to quit high school to go work in the canefields! . . ."

Carol pulls my sleeve. "That's enough," she says in English.

I go on for couple more minutes. Dead silence. They look away. Then Aunt Tomi says, "If it wasn't for your father, Yasuo here"—she nods toward her son—"wouldn't be alive today. When Yasuo came home from the war, he was near death with consumption. There were no medicines in Japan. I ask your father if he could buy some streptomycin in Hawaii. For a whole year we depended on his monthly shipment of streptomycin. It must've cost a fortune."

"*Okage sama de,*" Yasuo bows. He's now an Ito. Tomi gave him up to the Ito family after her brother Toru died and there was nobody to carry on the Ito line.

"What about your other sons?" I ask Tomi.

"Both Tadashi and Yasuo were wounded, Kaoru was killed in the Philippines," she says.

"My younger brother, Kiyoshi, was in the Philippines. As an interpreter. Was Kaoru in the Imperial Marines?"

I remember what Kiyo said about the atrocities committed by the marines in Manila.

"No, the Army."

Tadashi, Tomi's oldest son, comes over and puts his arm on my shoulder. "Come visit us. We have real peasants in Togo. It's only eighty kilometers. You'll like our farm."

It breaks the ice. *I like it when I don't hafta beg.*

"*Arigatoh,* but I'm very busy." I laugh.

The others laugh.

"Come on, you can spare a day." He pulls my arm like a kid. He's about my age. "I'll take you to your *furusato.*"

"What's that?" I mumble in English to Carol.

"Your ancestral home," Carol whispers.

"Where your mother and father were born," Tadashi says in Japanese.

Why I wanna go visit the home of failures? I oughta tell them grandfather was a thief!

Just then they page me on the loudspeaker and the bellhop brings me the phone, saying, "A call from Hawaii."

Chuck is on the other end. He says Barbara Hutton is

checking into a *ryokan* in Kyoto tomorrow. He wants me to get 6 dozen red roses to her room.

"Okay, Chuck." When I hang up, they all stare open-mouthed. *They must think I'm a big shot on a real busy schedule.*

"*Ojama shimashita,*" they say, and get up in a body and leave.

I feel kinda bad afterward, but I had to let them know I did it in spite of Papa and grandfather.

"You bad-mouthed Father, didn't you?" Mama says the next time I drop by Kahana. Papa bought a '52 Ford for $860 last year and built a garage from scrap lumber next to the house where we used to spar. It was money from Georgie's life insurance, which Mama bought when he went into the Army in '45. On maturity she asked Georgie to sign it over to her since she'd paid all the premiums. Once upon a time Georgie would have thought nothing of it. But now he had to explain to Gertrude that no, it wasn't because the folks disliked her, the insurance was theirs to begin with, he had not put in a cent.

Papa can hardly wait till July 30 when he'll be 65. Retirement is mandatory, so he can collect $27.71 weekly unemployment compensation for a year. It's the same as his ditchman's pay. The retirees use the money to visit Japan or the Philippines. Then he catches a cold in June. He cannot get rid of a cough. X-ray shows a spot. He has to go to Kula right away. He begs Dr. Blake to let him work 1½ months. He'll lose his unemployment if he goes out on medical.

"Being chief cook during the strike must've worn him down," Mama says.

"That's his *bachi* for showing off! He creates his own bad luck!" I tell her.

Miwa writes the family that Mama and Scott don't have enough to live on. We all chip in. Then I check with Happy's brother who works at the plantation office. He says Papa's pension and Social Security amount to what he made as ditchman; also Happy is presumed dead. I enclose a $50 bill in a sympathy card to his parents. The *koden* makes it official.

"Don't send Mama anymore, think of your own family first," I write my siblings.

The Senate finally passes the statehood bill. John Burns, the delegate to Congress, let Alaska go first, and his gamble pays off.

Hawaii ratifies statehood 132,938 to 7,854! The special election is set for a month later, July 28. Now the elected governor will have to answer to the voters. He'll have over 500 patronage jobs. Many Hawaiians oppose statehood. I don't blame them. First the haole planters kicked out Queen Liliuokalani and seized the government, then they got Hawaii annexed in 1898 to protect "American" interests in the wake of the Spanish-American War. Statehood will be the final nail in the coffin. One more thing, they'd lose all the patronage jobs they got under the territorial governor apppointed by the president. But how can they turn back the clock? The colonials are here to stay, and us their imported labor. They complain statehood means the niseis and the ILWU will dominate Hawaii. Back in April John Burns gave a speech at the ILWU convention in Seattle. He said the ILWU brought democracy to Hawaii. The papers accused Burns of being in Jack Hall's pocket. Hall bought a full-page ad in the Sunday paper saying the ILWU never asked favors from Burns.

But there are so many factions among the Democrats, it's hard to figure out who's with who. When Jack Hall quit the Democrats, he said he'd rather deal with a prostitute than a liberal because he knew where a prostitute stood. Now he and the ILWU support Hiram Fong, a Republican, for U.S. senator.

John Burns is a cinch, I think, but William Quinn upsets him 86,215 to 82,054. It's a fluke; Burns was so busy in Washington he never came back to campaign. But the rest of the voting don't make sense—Hiram Fong beats Frank Fasi (D) 87,175 to 77,692; Oren E. Long (D) beats Wilfred Tsukiyama for the other Senate seat; Dan Inouye (D) swamps Charles Silva (R) 111,733 to 51,058 for the lone House seat, and James Kealoha (R) beats Mitsuyuki Kido (D) for lieutenant governor. The Democrats control the state House 33 to 18, but the Republicans control the state Senate 14 to 11.

At 10:00 A.M. August 21 Hawaii becomes the fiftieth state, and church bells ring and people pour out into the streets. "Hey, we not second-class citizens no more," they say. "Hey, things gonna change at last."

Something else big is happening. They expanded the strip at the airport and Quantas and Pam Am are landing jets. Big hotels are going up in Waikiki. I take the family to watch the jets take off. When the first one looks like it's not going to make it, we tilt with it, Marcia runs. It clears the runway and we bust out laughing and clapping. United Airlines will be jetting to the West Coast in March.

In the old days people who went up Haleakala to Kula with T.B. never came back down. But now because of streptomycin most of the sanitarium is for mental patients. Scott drives Mama the 35 miles to Kula. Hachiro and Miwa take their car on alternate weekends.

In September I take the architect's exam the second time and pass history and theory, 3 hours, professional administration, 3 hours. It's 3 down and 4 to go. I enroll in another night course in engineering at UH.

23

Side Jobs

Ever since the Barbara Hutton job, Chuck takes a 4-month cruise every year. He calls it "study," which is tax deductible. So I get to do the program, schematic, prelim—the whole works. I get a raise to 14 Gs.

Dr. Hamada, a nisei dentist, hired Andrew Mori to design a $90,000 residence. He's not satisfied so he pays Mori and comes to us.

"You handle it," Chuck says, getting ready for his cruise. I enjoy the client meetings, sketching, developing the plans, and listening to what they're saying and not saying. Most people don't wanna be called stingy, so they use roundabout excuses to cut corners. You cannot blame them. It's the biggest investment of their lives. So you have to respect their budgets. Form follows function *and* budget. Arty designers, especially the ones right out of college, go way over budget and lose their commissions when they have to redraw. I have a big advantage—I can estimate the cost per square foot while sketching. And I don't hold back. That's the time to air out everything. Later misunderstandings cost too much. I try to sell them on natural wood, exposed structure, an honest and simple design. Anything extra is gravy. Dr. Hamada is happy with my design and working drawings. When the bids come in, the best qualified is only 5 Gs over budget! It's bullseye if you're within 10 percent.

At the Democratic convention in L.A. most of the Hawaii Democrats came out for Lyndon Johnson. Dan Inouye even made the nominating speech. But when John Kennedy got nominated, Jack Hall and the ILWU came out for Nixon. According to Lenny Imai, if Kennedy won he was going to appoint his brother as attorney general, and Bobby Kennedy was going after Jimmy Hoffa and the Teamsters. The Teamsters were the only union to stand by the ILWU during the Communist witch-hunt. Carol and I vote for Kennedy, but Nixon carries the outside-island ILWU vote and loses by only 115 votes, 92,410 to 92,295! Mama votes for Nixon too.

"Who told you? . . ." I ask her.

"Mr. Kometani. He drives all the union people to the courthouse."

"That's what the plantation bosses used to do with us!" I laugh. But I think afterward, *Jack Hall is smart. Political power is the only way you hold on to your gains.*

One day Jim Kawahara, a nisei lawyer, invites me to lunch. "I understand you did Dr. Hamada's house. Can you do a sixty-G job at chopped fee?"

"That's illegal," I say.

"It's against AIA rules, but not illegal. Everybody's doing it."

It's common knowledge. Many draftsmen use their bosses' seal to design residentials for a 3–5 percent fee. It saves the client 5–7 percent.

"I have a reputation to maintain," Chuck says when I ask him if I could use his seal and the office on nights and weekends.

"I didn't mean for free," I say, and peel off $300. "The going price is two hundred to two-fifty."

He takes the money and shuts up. Kawahara squeezes me down to 3.5 percent, $2,100. I finish it in a month working nights and weekends. The best bid is only 5 percent over budget.

When my house is going up in Makiki, Andrew Mori has a house going up 2 blocks away. Passersby go from one site to the other and compare our houses. My design is better. But I squeeze my ass; Mori's bound to find out. Kawahara's probably bragging how cheap he got me.

After the house is finished, Jim invites us to the house-warming. I've never been to any of Ames' housewarmings so I figure it's just another party like with the chug-a-lug contractors. The place is filled with nisei teachers, lawyers, and dentists. They're all wine-drinking college graduates!

Jim introduces me and right away they corner me. "So you're the architect. I like your exposed wood."

"And your space flows."

"Thanks."

"What school'd you go to?"

I mumble, "American School."

"Where's that?"

"Chicago."

"Is it part of the University of Chicago?"

"It's a correspondence school," I mumble, feeling like crawling into a hole.

"Oh."

They look away, smirk, and walk off. *Damn snobs!* Carol looks even more lost. What can she say to these snotty Bulaheads and Pakés? All she can talk about is family and wahine gossip. We leave after an hour, and I end up at the Columbia for straight shots of J&B.

Several months later I do a legit design of a 275-G home for Lowell Dillingham. After the bids are in, he decides not to build but instead renovate the old home. Chuck refuses to touch the old house. Nothing in it can be used, he says. Dillingham pays Chuck and goes to Mori. Mori cannot satisfy him so he pays Mori and begs Chuck to do a 150-G renovation. Chuck is leaving on another "study" cruise, so he sends me.

"Stick to French provincial since all their furnishing is French provincial," he says.

I'm having coffee on the lanai when I see Mori far down on the big lawn.

"What's he doing here?" I ask, worried.

"He's finishing the servants' quarters," Lowell says. "That's all he'll do."

Mori comes over to the lanai after Lowell leaves. He's one of the older niseis like Robert Kuni, the teacher back in Kahana.

"You better watch out about doing outside work." Mori shakes his finger like a schoolteacher.

"This not outside work."

"I don't mean this. There're lots of draftsmen doing petty stuff and using their bosses' rubber stamps."

"I work only for Ames."

"Nobody who does outside work will get a license," he says.

"I work only for Ames."

I feel so down afterward. I bet the shyster lawyer told him! Even the guys at Columbia laugh at me. "Only three and a half percent!? He wen catch you head! Chopped fee is five percent. Tell um that next time."

"That's what you get for bragging," Carol says.

"It's not bragging when I can . . ." *What's the use?*

In September I take the exam for the third time. I still feel pretty loose. I pass building construction and building equipment. Now comes the hard parts, site planning and structural design.

Soon afterward Bob Agena, the contractor I used for most of the jobs and Jim Kawahara's house, asks me to design an 80-G house. When it's nearly finished, I ask Papa to write the character *kotobuki* (long life) on a 3′ × 3′ tracing paper. I have the character carved into a *kamban*-like ornamented board to be hung on a post at the walk to the front door.

It's a nicer housewarming party. There're carpenters and plumbers and electricians with a smattering of high *maka-maka* college punks. All us noncollege types chug-a-lug whiskey while the wine drinkers stay in their own group. But sooner or later one of them comes up. "I like your design. What school'd you go to?"

"American School," I mumble.

"Where's that?"

"It's a correspondence school in Chicago." I look off, cringing.

"Good job," he says, and moves away.

Several months later Bob calls me. "You know a wahine used to be called Margaret Doi? She Mrs. Omi now from Kauai, but she says she knows you."

"Yeah, we from the same stinking plantation camp."

"Well, she came to the house with my sister. When I told her you designed the house, she said, 'Cannot be! Steven must be Kiyoshi! Toshio was a garbage collector! You're sure it's Toshio and not Kiyoshi? I never thought Toshio would amount to anything. He was such a braggart!' How come she no like you so much? I bet you wen throw one pass at her, eh?"

"Naw, I wen dance with her only once."

"Well, anyway, she get no use for you."

"I don't know why, but people love to run me down. And I never did nothing to them."

Peter Doi and I now play tag. He spies me and runs through Woolworths and I chase through the store and out the alley.

"Hey, Peter!" We're both puffing. "Hey, Pete, you a lawyer yet?"

"Naw."

"Lemme know, yeah? I really need a lawyer. I figure I can trust a hometown boy."

"Yeah."

24

Spoiled Brat

Papa gets lucky again. He gets out of Kula Sanitarium in July. Streptomycin cures him in 20 months. Georgie sends them round-trip tickets to California to celebrate his discharge. They spend the night with us, and Carol fixes a buffet of sushi, *nishime,* and store-bought *kalua* pig and *lomi-lomi* salmon.

We take our plates into the parlor and sit on the couch in front of the TV. The teenagers, Danny, Marcia, and their uncle, Scott, form a circle on the floor. Chrys and Gerald stay in the kitchen. Danny and Marcia horse around and chatter-chatter while Scott is so serious. You can tell who's *sansei* and who's nisei. But Scott sounds and looks so much like Kiyo. They have Mama's jaw and long face. Danny and Marcia have Carol's round face.

"Joji is prospering, he's already built five rentals," Mama says.

"The Oyama children are hard workers, unlike their father . . ." I stare at the old man but he's got a thick skin.

Then Mama says they're all going on to Louisville, Kentucky after visiting California, since Ann is expecting her second child. Her first child, Patti, born couple years back, had the same turned-in left foot like Marcia. But they were able to fix it right away with heavy casts, which they changed every few weeks. The plantation hospital is primitive compared to the mainland.

"Where did you get the money to go to Kentucky?" I ask Mama.

"Kiyoshi sent us," Mama says.

"He sent you money to go to Kentucky?"

"No, it was money for Father's Japan trip."

"You don't want to go to Japan?" I ask him. Every *issei* dreams of going back.

"No, I'd rather go to Kentucky," he says with a wave of his hand.

"What did Kiyo say?"

"He says it's up to me," Papa says.

"You've never been back to Japan in what . . ."

"Fifty-one years."

"And you'd rather go to Kentucky instead? Is Kiyo going to send you some more money for Japan?"

"No, he said Kentucky will be the same as a Japan trip," Mama says.

"But why? You don't care if you never go back? What if you don't have another chance?"

Finally Mama lets the cat out of the bag. Brian Kono's oldest sister is married to the famous surgeon, Doc Sawada. He visited Papa often at Kula. When she learned Papa was going to California, Mrs. Sawada drove all the way from Wailuku to Kahana.

"As long as you're going to the mainland, why don't you go on to Kentucky to see your daughter? Tsune-chan will be overjoyed. You haven't even met my little brother or your granddaughter," she said. When Papa hesitated she said, "If it's the money, don't worry. We'll pay your plane fare."

"No, we have the money. We were thinking of going to Kentucky," Papa said.

"Why didn't you say, 'Yes, we don't have the money'!? You only get into trouble when you act rich," I say.

He laughs, "Heh-heh."

When doing the dishes, Mama asks Carol if we can board Scott next year so he can attend UH.

"We'll pay you twenty-five dollars a month. He wants to be an architect," she says.

I'm in bed when Carol tells me. I fly to their bedroom. "Cannot! I cannot put up Jun!"

"Why do you hate Jun so much?" Mama says, and I hit the roof again!

"I don't hate him! In fact I like him! But my family comes first! Danny will be going to college next year! I'm going to be helping Fujie's nephew next year too!"

"You help outsiders before your own family?"

"His father loaned me money to buy this house when even the banks refused me! I owe them more than I owe you!"

"Don't worry, I'll ask Kiyoshi."

"I cannot help Jun! I'm struggling! I don't even have an architect's license. Raising children is like buying insurance! If you're good to them, they'll pay you back! What did you do for me!? You made me quit high school! You made me work in the canefields! I went to night school for my diploma! You didn't do a thing for me! Because of you I now have to compete with college graduates fifteen years younger! And you want to pile some more on me! I'm finished with you! I sacrifice ten years! . . ."

I'm so steamed I cannot sleep. I feel so tired the next morning when I drive them to the airport. I have to settle down and focus on the exam.

I write Kiyo, "Watch out, Mama is desperate. She wants to ramrod Scott through college. They're scared they got nobody to look after them in their old age!"

Kiyo and Audrey divorced couple years back. I could've told him no haole woman is going to stick with a starving playwright. Even a nisei wahine would throw in the towel. I felt sad. It was the first divorce in the family. Besides, I liked Audrey. She was a good wife. Then Kiyo came out to San Francisco to teach at S.F. City College.

Couple days later Danny says he's not going to be an architect. "You think me *pupule*, go compete with a father and two uncles?"

But I soon forget the old farts. Out of sight, out of mind. I cram and cram till my head feels like cement. I have only site and structural left, but there's a rumor they're going to make everybody retake the whole test every year beginning 1962. *I'll give up if they do that. Damn Chuck, he pulling for me to fail!* "*Architecture is a gentleman's profession,*" *he says. But the other bosses, they support their boys. According to my "pals" at the Columbia, Andrew Mori said nobody without college will get a license.*

It's like I have a main-event bout every September. The previous 8 months are preparation for it. The day before the 5-hour structural design exam, I come home late, thinking, *Shit, I gotta cram some more.* Carol has dinner ready. A fat, unopened letter addressed only to me from Betty is on the table. She usually addresses it Mr. and Mrs. Steven Oyama.

Betty's note (she's the only one in the family with bad penmanship) says, "I'm sending your copy ahead of Papa and Scott so that you won't blow up at them like Georgie and Trudy."

Enclosed are 4 typewritten pages, single spaced.

Dear Oyamas:

The purpose of this letter is in regard to Scott's education which involves all the Oyama children. Scott is determined to become an architect. At his age such determination should be encouraged. We have talked to him and have confidence in his ability to succeed.

Being interested in architecture, he does not have a free choice of schools since most schools do not have a complete curricula which will give him a well-rounded education. Of the architectural schools considered, we have narrowed it down to three—Univ. of Cincinnati, Univ. of Illinois, and Univ. of Mich. Of these three, Univ. of Cincinnati is most desirable because of its comprehensive curricula and especially its cooperative program. The cooperative program is a plan whereby a student goes to school part-time and works part-time, with full pay. The job is guaranteed by the school to be in line with his training as an architect. Because of this part-time plan, he goes to school for six years.

The financial situation for Scott's education is as follows:

(1) $2,000 savings by Mom and Dad

(2) $1,500 from insurance maturing at age 22 (to pay for years 5 & 6)

Obviously, Scott cannot go through school without financial aid to supplement the wages from the cooperative plan plus items 1 and 2 above. To assure his continuous schooling without interruption due to financial deficiencies, he needs commitments from his family.

All of his brothers and sisters are happy to know that Scott wants to make something of himself, and we all indicate willingness to give him room and board, but this is unfeasible because of the lack of architectural colleges in proximity to our homes. We are in a sense all dreamers offering support though nothing concrete. A college education cannot be paid for by sentiment and dreams. I think for Scott's sake we *must* be practical.

After talking to Mom and Pop, there is no doubt in my mind that each of the Oyama families, including myself, is not flowing with money. Therefore, one or two of the Oyama children should not and possibly cannot meet the brunt of the financial responsibility. Since Scott is the last one, this is the least we can do as a group, for the sake of the family. Furthermore, none of us now have to support Mom and Pop—as is the case in many families—because they are self-sufficient in that they receive support from Social Security and pension. Therefore, small percentages of our salaries given to Scott would be meeting part of our responsibilities.

Brian has said many times that we should help Scott, but I cannot ask Brian to help without some embarrassment and hesitation on my part, if Scott's other brothers and sisters refuse. This is why I say his education should be a family project, and I would think we all *want* it to be a family project—I do and feel very strongly about it because I think highly of Scott and want to see him get ahead. Sure, it takes sacrifices on all our parts, but I personally feel it's worth it. Everybody's finances are low. The Brian Konos are no exception. We don't have a cent (literally) in our savings account, and we had to borrow $3,000 on a long-term basis from the Kono brothers to buy our house. But if we care enough about Scott, I'm sure we can all chip in.

Helping Scott through school to obtain a Bachelor in Arch. or any other profession of his choice can be looked upon as a noble deed by everyone who helps him. There is, however, another aspect of the deed which is overlooked. If Scott does not have a college education and is consequently deprived of the chance to establish himself firmly in a profession, the family will somehow some time in the future be burdened by his lack of profession. If he is helped through college and obtains a degree, his chance of success in his field of choice will be assured. After successfully establishing himself, he can be considered an asset to you and the family as a whole because there will now be an addition in the financial resources within the family to cope with family crisis, which seems to be inevitable in all families. In this philosophy there is an assurance that in time of crisis there would be multiple shoulders to lean on. Helping Scott then is to assure such a state.

"Goddam spoiled brat!" I so angry I shake!
"What's the matter?" Carol says.
The last page reads:

154

Attached are breakdown of expenses:

Account of finances as it would be if Scott goes to
        Univ. of Cincinnati
Trip fare and expenses from Maui to Cincinnati
Approximately $400—most of this will be earned
        by Scott during the summer of 1962

1. Freshman year, 1962–63
   Expenses
        $1850—Tuition (750), books (100), room & board
                estimate from catalog (1000)
         $250—Misc. meals on Sundays, entertainment, etc.
        $2100—Amount needed
   Available
        $2000—Savings from Mom and Dad
        Unaccounted amount needed = $100

2. Second through fourth year of schooling, 1963–66
   Expenses per year
        $2100—Total expenses as indicated above
        −1200—Earnings expected thru the Cooperative plan
          900—Total expenses per year
           x3—3 yrs from 2nd to 4th years
        $2700—Total expenses unaccounted for 1963–66
          100—For freshman year (see above)
        $2800—Total for lst, 2nd, 3rd, & 4th years

3. Apportionment of $2800 for 4 years (1962–66) among family
        members: 2800 divided by 4 = 700 per year
   Suggestion No. 1
        1. 3 brothers: 2/3 of 700 = $468/yr divided by 3 =
            $156 per brother per yr
        2. 3 sisters: 1/3 of 700 = $232/yr divided by 3 = $77
            per sister per yr (divided by 12 = $6.42 per sister
            per month)
   Suggestion No. 2
        3 bros. and 3 sis. = 6
        700 divided by 6 = $117 per family per yr for 4 yrs
        (divided by 12 = $9.75 per month for 4 yrs)

Suggestion No. 3
> If it is impossible for any one family to contribute toward
> Scott's education, perhaps the difference can be absorbed by
> others who are in more favorable position. In such a case the
> above figures can be used as a guide to determine what the
> difference is.

I throw the papers in the air. "Spoiled brat! Phi Beta Kappa,
shit! Spoiled brat! She wen catch all the gravy! Now the old futts
wanna suck some more blood! 'Scott is determined to become an
architect.' I bet the old futts wen push him to leapfrog over me
and Georgie! He still got one more year of high school! Why the
hell they *shimpai* so much!?"

Danny says, "I think I go into commercial art or electronic
engineering. Too many architects in this family already."

"You think UH going to admit you!? They don't take "C"
students!"

"I changed my mind about medicine," Marcia, who's an "A"
student, says. "I'll be an old maid by the time I finish my residence."

Fickle wahines!

" 'Educate the boys!' I told Mama and Papa over and over.
'The girls not going pay you back! They going get married!' All I
got was smart answers. I started working at fourteen! I was twenty-
two when I asked permission to marry. 'You're too young. You
have to help the family,' they said. So we gave all of Carol's pay-
check to Mama plus one-third of mine. Right, Ma?"

"That's right," Carol says.

"I bet you Mama will deny it today! Damn bloodsuckers!
They go all the way to Kentucky just to impress the Konos, and
they think nothing of asking for more money! For what!? Another
trip to Kentucky!? I disowned them fifteen years ago!"

Danny jumps to leave.

"Sit down!"

"I finish already."

"I not finished. You too, Marcia."

"Yes, sit for a while," Carol says. "You people can't sit still
for a minute."

"You guys are lucky compared to what I went through! I

had to quit high school! I went to work in the canefields when I was sixteen! Papa was six thousand in the hole. He expected us—"

"I wen hear the story already," Danny mumbles.

"You hear but you no listen!" I wag a finger. "You no believe me! You don't know how lucky you are! I fighting for my life! I still one plantation boy! I trying to get out! I doing it all for you! You should help me! At least show appreciation! I had to quit high school! I—"

"Ma, can I go?" little Chrys says in her tiny voice.

"Yes."

"Excuse me," she says. We watch her walking up the steps to the split level over the garage as Danny moves toward the door.

"You know, I never wen ask to be born. Why you wen born me if you going talk li'dat?" he says.

"You lucky *I* wen born you instead of Grampa!" I yell, but he slips out before I finish.

"You have to calm down. You have some studying to do," Carol says.

"Shit! I lost my appetite."

I get up and pour a glassful of J&B.

"Don't drink any more."

I take a swig and get madder. *Damn kids! I busting my ass for them and they take it for granted!*

"Why don't you take a nap. Sleep it off. I'll wake you."

"Yeah."

I get up at 3 and cram till 8, my head pounding.

The 5-hour structural engineering exam starts at 9. I feel so tense and angry. *Shit! the spoiled brat!* When I read the first problem, the words float away. *Concentrate! Concentrate! I wen do these duck-soup problems over and over in practice! They call them gym fighters who leave their best fights in the gym. . . .*

By the time I make sense of the words 2 hours are gone! I rush in a panic the next 3 hours. *Damn! I always playing catch-up!* I finish in time but as soon as I walk out, it hits me in the guts! I remember my stupid mistakes! *What the hell I thinking of!?*

"I goofed on the first two problems. Ninety-nine percent of the time I can do them with my eyes closed," I tell Carol. "What was I doing? My mind was somewhere else."

"Awateboh."

"Is this what they mean by 'cracking up?' I so angry, I no can think."

"I think you better write Ann right away. Get it off your chest before the next test."

"I too tired."

"Tomorrow maybe."

I fall asleep and wake up, my body screaming for more booze. *Damn Ann!*

"Don't drink anymore. Take a day off. Go get a *shiatsu*," Carol says.

Couple days later, I write on a yellow legal pad with 5 carbons for the other siblings.

Dear Ann,

Hope all is well. We are in good health.

The engineering exam is over and encl. are the problems of the exam and the requirements to qualify to take the exam. When you're through, send it to Georgie. This is nationally recognized.

Received your outline letter on Scott's education. I was pretty upset! Received it the day before my engineering exam. I am still mad! I was so mad I goofed!

There are many things I am going to set you straight. You have been very fortunate among the Oyamas so I will start from the beginning.

The folks and I never seen eye to eye for over 20 years except of late. Papa compared to his children wasn't a hard worker. Papa actually couldn't afford more than 3 kids but he had 7 and luckily all of them good children.

Papa really likes to talk and drink. At heart he is a country clown but there are many good things about him and he is our father. Mama is more serious and would give you a "sob story" every time. She sure took a lot from Papa—you weren't even born yet! Today you look at Mama and Papa—Mama is the boss and backbone!

"Educate the boys! You're going to depend on *them!*" I kept telling them. You know what they said? "You *ni ga haru,*" "Look at the other no. 1 sons," "Don't worry, we won't depend on you . . ."

I fill out 3 more pages of what Danny Kenji calls my "broken record." "I have to keep telling you because you don't listen!" I keep yelling. "Maybe he'll listen if you were sober and weren't so angry," Carol said.

. . . Your estimate on Scott's education is very conservative. Most parents tell me it costs $2500 to $3000 p/yr. I don't know about the others but I will not commit myself. My children come first. If things look bright I can send Scott $100 for Xmas.

One may wonder why I pursue to be a registered architect. It's my old age insurance—being registered does not mean you're going to make money. In fact here we call it a "certificate to starvation!" As I get older, it's tougher all around bucking college kids all the time.

I am really a tired man with studying, working, and running around on my side jobs. I don't even have time for my family. Hope someday I make it and all the Oyamas can pool their resources as architects—wishful thinking but possible.

My best and most—

Steve

Saying it in good English is like pulling your punches. You cannot let go BANG! with your pidgin anger.

Four days later I take the 5-hour site planning exam. The problem is to design an airport.

"I think I did okay," I tell Carol, "but site is real subjective. Depends on the curve, and how I did in my engineering."

A week later we get a letter from Ann: she apologizes for the bad timing of the letter; she's well aware of the hardships I went through; and Scott will have to work his way since we're all struggling.

Betty writes a 5-page letter: Ann's baby is late so Mama is staying over in Kentucky. Papa and Scott are flying back and going directly from the airport to Maui so they won't be stopping over.

All the misunderstanding was her fault.

Georgie and Trudy had sent the folks $500 for their first trip to the mainland. Georgie was so proud. He wanted to show off his success. He didn't even want to share the folks with Betty's family. She and her family need not come to the L.A. Airport, he said. "We haven't seen them in over six years!" she pleaded. He relented, but he tried to freeze out her family in entertaining them. Papa, Mama, and Scott then spent a week with Morris in San Francisco. When they got back, Mama said they weren't going home, but to Kentucky since Ann was having her second child. "We wouldn't have sent you the $500 if we knew you were that rich! You fooled us!" Georgie and Gertrude exploded.

Except for the copy mailed to Morris in San Francisco, Scott was supposed to hand deliver the other copies of Ann's letter. Betty and Yukio were still reading their copy when Georgie and Trudy came storming into their house.

"You think we owe you a college education!? Georgie and I are struggling!" Trudy yelled at Scott.

"You take my handout and you ask for more!" Georgie yelled.

"We could have used the five hundred dollars," Trudy said.

"Why didn't you stay home and work instead of gallivanting to Kentucky!? I'm through with you people! I did enough already! I hope Steve tells you off!" Georgie said.

"What are they saying?" Papa asked Betty in Japanese.

"*Nan de mo nai,*" Betty said. "It's nothing. Pretend you don't understand." He looked so sad, Betty didn't want to spoil his vacation.

Georgie came to get Scott early next morning. "You wanna be an architect? I'll teach you. I'll make a man out of you."

He was building another house and he had Scott hold up frames and pound nails. "You can get a degree but you don't know how to get along with contractors! I know more about machine shop than you'll ever learn! . . ." It went on for a week.

Instead of Scott delivering my copy of Ann's letter, Betty mailed it to me, hoping to prevent *my* blowing up and spoiling

Papa's vacation. Getting it a week earlier would give me time to cool off, she thought. The one nice thing was that Papa and Scott were able to visit with her family, as Georgie and Trudy didn't want anything more to do with them.

Carol reads the letter and laughs. "It's just like the Oyamas. Up-and-down, up-and-down, worry-worry, you can't sit still. Without the Nakama blood Danny, Marcia, and Chrys would be jumpier than they are!"

Ann's baby boy arrives 3 weeks late. Mama catches the plane to Los Angeles, rests a day in Pocomo, and flies into Honolulu.

"Tsuneko's letter caused a lot of trouble," I tell her, driving back from the airport.

"It's all in the family so it's all right, *ne?*"

"I cannot help Jun. My family comes first. Jun can work his way."

"But none of the *sansei*s are working their way."

"Look at Anshan's children. Chiaki worked all night at a bakery, even supported his family and got an engineering degree."

"Anshan was a drunk," she says.

"What does his being a drunk have to do with it!?" I'm out of control again! All she does is press a button! "He was a drunk, but he didn't leave his children with a six thousand-dollar debt!"

"You didn't pay off the debt, Kiyoshi did."

"But you took ten years of my life! You and Papa are parasites! You're terrified now there's nobody to look after you in your old age! That's why you want to push Jun through college at our expense!"

"Don't worry, we won't depend on you."

"Shit!" I rev the engine and screech into 9th Avenue, and swerve into the driveway at full speed. Zukkkk! Carol runs out.

"What's the matter!?"

I slam the door. "You drive her to the airport tomorrow! She drives me nuts!"

Three weeks later I get the results of the exam in the mail. I flunk both exams. Ames is all smiles.

25

Governor John Burns

The board passes a ruling effective this year saying that applicants who do not show improvement on their exams will not be allowed to take the test the following year, but it's not retroactive so I'm saved for the time being.

I do a design for Anna Hagen. Then another one for another of Chuck's millionaire friends. I now do nearly everything with just one draftsman—program, prelim, building permit, etc. I put it out to bid and even put out a schedule to coordinate the electrician, plumber, and carpenter so that there'll be no time wasted, like the electrician waiting for the plumber to finish. Chuck brings in the jobs and does the billing.

I do couple more side jobs—a Dr. Miyamoto, M.D., and Mr. Taira of Taira Stores. Many niseis are now middle class.

"You shouldn't take any more side jobs till you get your license," Carol says.

"We need the money. The Chevy is falling apart. Besides, they like my designs. They keep asking me."

I'm so rushed, what with working, doing side jobs, studying, and taking classes, I need *shiatsu* 2–3 times a week. Old Osato is nearly blind but his fingers can dig down into my tired bones. Lying on my stomach, I talk about the old farts forcing me to quit school, etc., etc. I cannot get it out of my system.

"All I want is for him to apologize."

Osato laughs. "He'll never do that. He'll send his servant to apologize for him."

"Why?"

"That's Bushido. *Bushi ni wa nigon nashi.* A samurai sticks to his word. The opposite of that is he never apologizes."

"That's right! That's why he's so tight-lipped. He's afraid he might promise something he cannot back up. Are you from samurai family?"

He laughs. "No."

"Why do all these peasants act like samurais?"

"You can pretend to be anything in Hawaii."

West Maui used to be so depressed, but now all the Kahana wives work at the new Maui Sheraton Hotel. Other hotels are going up and Tatsuo Hirano, a local contractor, hires guys from Kahana 3:30 to 7:00 on weekdays and all day on weekends. The Big 5 get competition from Chinn Ho and big mainland developers. New hotels go up in Waikiki and Ala Moana.

Chuck sends me out to collect final payments now. One haole lady says she's broke. "Take it out on me," she says. "She must be at least eighty!" I tell Chuck. We now demand payment before completion from rich widows.

Scott and Danny graduate high school in June. Scott leaves for Pocomo, where Yukio, now a supervisor at Johns Mansville, gets him a summer job. He'll stay with Yukio and Betty and leave for Eugene, Oregon in the fall. UH has no architecture, law, or medical schools. The Univ. of Oregon gives free tuition to Hawaii residents. Danny horsed around so much in high school, he barely gets admitted to UH. Marcia will be a junior at Kaimuki High. All the massaging of her foot pays off. She walks without a limp.

September finally arrives. I have two 5-hour exams left. The first is for structural engineering. My head is clear. The problems are easy.

"I think I passed it," I tell Carol.

Two days later it's site planning. The problem is to design a yacht harbor.

"I did okay, I think. But it's so subjective. Depends on whether Andy Mori is targeting me."

Several weeks later I learn I pass structural and flunk site.

"I'm taking two weeks off," I tell Chuck. "I gotta get away and rest my head."

It's our first ride on a jet. The 8½ hour flight is now 4½.

We fly to Detroit, buy a Dodge Dart, and drive back, stop at Yellowstone, Yosemite, Reno, then ship the car back from San Francisco. It saves us $300.

Kiyo lives in a run-down neighborhood on Golden Gate Avenue and teaches history at S.F. City College while writing plays.

"Ann and I lived in a mixed neighborhood in D.C.," he says.

Low rent, I nearly blurt.

He looks different. Not as skinny.

"You put on weight."

"Yeah, I quit smoking."

"Yeah? How come?"

"My luck's so bad I figure I gotta last."

"That's what you should do," Carol says to me.

"Cannot. I've got too much pressure. How d'you do it?"

"Wasn't easy. I'd quit for a week and say, 'I can do it,' and go out and buy a pack and chain-smoke the whole thing. Happened four-five times. I used to dream about cigarettes."

"I smoke a pack a day, easy. Some days two. I'm hooked."

"That's why you're so hyper," Carol says.

I laugh. "That's why I need my booze."

He takes us to Mingei-ya, a rustic Japanese restaurant. It's just like the restaurants in Japan.

"Damn Ann set me back a whole year! I'm still mad!" I say after several *sakes*.

"What a stupid letter, no?" Carol says.

"It's the academic mind. It solves problems by the book, but I think most of the letter was Brian's—"

"You mean he wrote it?" I cut in.

"No, the phrasing was Ann's, but I think the ideas were Brian's. After all, Ann was expecting any minute and was in no condition to think things through. Brian grilled Papa about his finances. Papa told Mama afterward he felt like he was led onto the scaffold for a hanging."

"I could've told him Papa don't have a pot to piss in!"

"Yeah, but imagine being found out by an outsider. He was so mad he said he'd never visit Ann and Brian again."

"Mama told you this?"

"No, Betty, though she didn't know exactly why he was so mad."

"Well, he's got a short temper and a short memory. That's the trouble with Bulaheads, they don't remember their screw-ups."

"Mama asked me when they visited, 'What are we going to do about Jun's education?' I thought there was a school of architecture at the University of Louisville, where Brian taught, so I told her to ask Ann. I feel sorry for Scott. He knows nothing about our family history. I told him, 'Why don't you go into some other field? You'll be competing with Steve and Georgie if you go into architecture.' He said, 'I like buildings.' He must've thought he could help you both if he got an architect's license."

"Naw, Mama pushed him. She wants to ramrod him through. She and Papa are desperate. The plantation is phasing out Kahana. Practically all the *luna*s and Okinawans have left already. There are lots of empty houses. I keep telling them, 'I bet you'll be the last ones to leave. You people have no *hilahila*.' "

"Where did the *luna*s and Okinawans go?"

"The *luna*s bought land in Honokawai and built their own houses. The Okinawans left for Honolulu."

"So what'll happen to the people that's left?"

I shrug. "I'm thinking of doing another addition to my place. Not right away. I'll have a dry run and invite them for Christmas. I'm not going to tell them to stay with me until I break them in. Under one condition. If they get sick, you, me, and Georgie share medical bills. If they get senile it's the old age home, I mean if they get past eighty. Some of them pretty alert at eighty-five. It's just a thought. Maybe in a couple of years . . ."

Kiyo drives us back in his '52 Plymouth to the hotel and walks us to the lobby.

Suddenly I feel real low. "You know, I'm real tired, I've been hustling for sixteen years and I'm still at the same place. Now I'm competing with guys half my age. I might as well resign myself to being a plantation boy the rest of my life."

"No give up. If Frank Lloyd Wright had died at fifty, he'd be unknown today. All his breaks came after he was fifty. It started with the Tokyo earthquake and the Imperial Hotel," he says.

"Well, Frank Lloyd Wright didn't have Andrew Mori targeting him."

"You'll outlast him," he says.

"He won't be chairman of the board next year," Carol says.

"By the way, d'you know there's diabetes in our family?" Kiyo says.

"You take insulin?" Carol says. "My brother, Tenki, is a Type I diabetic."

"No, I control it by diet. But some days I get so tired I have to go lie down in the middle of the day and I can't get up for days. Remember how I always ran out of gas in the ring? The third round was murder. I could never figure out why. I thought I wasn't training hard enough. But you oughta go take a glucose test."

"I'm okay."

"But he craves alcohol," Carol says.

"Me too," Kiyo says. "I get real shaky when I get hungry. Liquor is quick energy."

Carol laughs. "I was going to talk to you about Steve's drinking problem!"

"It's in the genes," Kiyo says. "I drink like a fish too."

"I'm okay," I say. It's the last thing I wanna hear. I get enough handicaps. "Hey, why donchu come back to Hawaii. You can get a better job."

"Naw, I feel free out here. Besides, I like the fog."

The Republicans are so out of touch they accuse John Burns of being soft on communism. They don't realize the issue is dead as a doorknob. But the big race is for the Senate seat vacated by Oren E. Long. It's Ben Dillingham II vs. Congressman Dan Inouye. We watch their debate on TV. They're like Mutt and Jeff. Like me and Chuck. Inouye is 5'6", Ben 6'3", 250 lbs. I met Ben several times and he's real nice and not spoiled as people say, but I'm for the Bulahead. Thirty-five percent of the registered voters are Bulaheads and 90 percent of them vote Democratic. The majority of part-Hawaiians and Filipinos vote Democratic too. And you can count on the ILWU to deliver the plantation votes on the outside islands. Inouye swamps Dillingham, and Burns beats Quinn 114,000 to 82,000 for governor. But it means nothing if I don't get my license. Without it I'm Chuck's houseboy.

Everybody talks about the "1954 revolution" when the Democrats took over the legislature. They forget the real revolution took place in the canefields when the ILWU broke the monopoly of the Big 5. Politics was the by-product.

26

Sixth Try

I enroll in another night class in site planning. It was only a 5-hour test so I never took it seriously. "You know," I tell Carol, "I'm glad I flunked site. I used to think it was easy so I didn't give it a second thought. . . ."

Eleven of us started out in 1958. Four passed, and 1 left for the states, so there are 6 left, but there're about 10 others with only site to go. I don't know if Mori is targeting me but he's making me a better site planner. This year he's not the chairman.

Then I throw a fit one morning. The *Advertiser* says the Registration Board wants to revise the standards! Those who don't pass in 2 tries will have to retake the whole exam! I ask Kiyo to write me a 3-minute speech for the public hearing:

1. We are not schoolkids, we work and study so leniency must be given.
2. If anyone gets a low grade—suspend him for a year and a year later he must show proof that he has studied.
3. What about design (12 hrs) and site (5 hrs)? These are so optional, no criteria.
4. What about those that have only 1 part left—do they have to repeat all over? If that's the case might as well tell all the registered architects to retake the exam too.
5. If this is passed, 99 percent of the applicants will be repeating the entire exam.

(Don't make it so it will irritate the board).

Ames is all smiles when he shows up. *Damn bastard jinxing me!*

On Friday Ames calls and says a Mr. and Mrs. Hampton will be showing up at the office tomorrow morning at 9. They're from Washington, D.C., and are thinking of transferring to Hawaii.

"Will you show them around?"

Saturday mornings are my free time for study!

"Shouldn't take a couple of hours," he says.

"What's his budget?"

"I don't know."

"What does he do?"

"Works for the government."

"They're your friends?"

"Friends of friends. They're from North Carolina originally."

I'm already pissed when they come in at 9 sharp. Ed is 50ish, tall, broad, with brown horned-rimmed glasses, droopy eyes, reddish moustache and beard. Doris is slight and stooped.

"What price range are you looking for?"

Ed strokes his beard and laughs apologetically. "Well . . . may we see what you have?"

We make small talk as I drive them to Manoa. He's been 25 years with GSA and wants to live in Hawaii when he retires. He would have to take a pay cut if he comes out here even with the cost of living allowance.

I take him to Lowell Dillingham's. He inspects the house carefully.

"Can we look inside?"

"I don't think they're up yet."

When I quote the price, he strokes his beard and nods and nods, laughing. "Ahhh . . . it's out of our range."

"What's your budget?"

He strokes again, ponders, and laughs. "Well, we're flexible. . . . We want to leave open the options."

I drive them to Keith Reynolds'.

"I don't know him so I can't show you the inside. This one was $500,000 back in 1950."

He inspects it for another 30 minutes.

We go next to Anna Hagen's. "This was $200,000 couple of years ago."

Anna comes to the door when I knock. "Hello, Steve." I explain the situation. "Oh, sure," she says, and lets us in.

Ed inspects every detail with Doris right behind him.

"I used to inspect buildings," he says.

"Were you a building inspector?"

"No, on my job with GSA."

He takes so much time I want to apologize to Anna.

Finally we get out and Ed shakes as he lets out that hic-cupy laugh. "Hmmm . . . I'm afraid it's over our budget."

"So what's your budget?" I keep myself from yelling.

"Hmmm . . . How does $100,000 sound?"

It's noon when we drive out of Manoa. I take him to Dr. Hamada's. "This was $90,000 in 1960."

He does his inspection. "Does that include the land?"

"Land is extra. It sells by the square foot here, ten to twenty-five dollars per depending on the location. This lot was fifty thousand."

He laughs. "Heh-heh-heh-heh. My one hundred thousand has to cover both land and building."

I drive to Bob Agena's Japanese-style house in Kapahulu.

"This one was sixty thousand, land was forty thousand three years ago."

"Hmmm . . . Did Charles do this?"

"No I did."

"Hmmm . . . What are your credentials?"

"WHAT!?"

"What schools did you attend."

"I not architect yet."

"Hmmm . . ." He nods and nods, stroking his beard. "So, you're a draftsman?" He waits.

"Yeah."

"And Charles lets you design houses?"

"I pay him three hundred for use of his seal."

"Hmmm . . . Sounds highly unethical."

Just then Agnes Agena comes out with women from her coffee klatch. She waves and I wave back as the other women look at us, chirping like sparrows. I check my watch. It's 1:30! *Damn, my whole morning's shot!*

"Why are there so many Japs?"

"What!?"

"Why are there so many Japs?"

"Shit! The plantations wen bring our parents to work the canefields! We born here! We fought the Japs and the Nazis! We only thirty-five percent of the population, but we took eighty percent of Hawaii's casualties! We wen earn the right to be here! We wen work and die for it! You no can afford Chuck or me! Go hunt for bargains someplace else!"

Agnes and her friends are staring at me. *I don't care.*

I drive breakneck, jamming the brake at every stop. I let them off at the Royal Hawaiian.

Monday morning Chuck is in early. He calls me into his office.

"You know, Steve, the first rule of business is, 'Don't insult your client.' "

"They're not clients, they're bargain hunters. That's why you dumped them on me." *You sic them on me on my day off so I no can study! You scared to death I gonna pass the test!*

"Still, you have to be civil."

"He called me a Jap."

"I've heard you call people that."

"It's different when *I* say it."

"Lots of times it's only used as an abbreviation, like calling a Scotsman a Scot. No offense is intended."

"Not the way he said it."

At the public hearing over 40 of us get up to the microphone and give our 3-minute speeches. Others ask why Hawaii don't have reciprocity; Hawaii's standards are a holdover from the old Big 5 days to keep out mainland competition; it's a conspiracy of the haole majority on the board to keep out the nisei, who are now 25 percent of the architects; even the licensed architects from the mainland flunk the test. After 3 hours, Martin Van Dresser, the chairman, says it's only a proposal, it needs further study.

Masato Nakamura was the first to pass out of the 11 of us in the "class of '58." He did it on his second try. He had his own business for a while but works now in the comptroller's office in the state government.

"Don't worry, Steve, they won't change the standards. They can't get more restrictive when everybody else is getting more liberal," he says at lunch. "Besides, Governor Burns says he wants to see the nisei make it. Quinn used only mainland architects."

I gotta relax. I'm too close to give up, but there're 10 other guys, all college grads, with only site left. What chance have I got? My back is stiff as a board. It gives me the trots.

Finally September arrives. The test for site is on the fourth and last day. The problem is a shopping center, and inside it, a supermarket like Safeway. I studied many shopping centers on the mainland. Everywhere I went I took photos. I forget the tension once I get into it. I finish it ahead of time, review it, and hand it in.

"I think I passed," I tell Carol, "but it depends on how the other ten guys did and how much Mori hates me."

I take the night off and visit the Columbia.

"You wen pass?" they ask me.

"I'm keeping my fingers crossed."

"How d'you feel about it?" Lenny Imai asks.

"I feel pretty good. I'm going to hire a lawyer if they flunk me this time. Site is so damn subjective."

"That's to keep it exclusive," Lenny says. "Architecture never existed as a profession till the early 1900s. Frank Lloyd Wright trained as an engineer. They didn't have architecture schools in those days. Even now you don't need architects. Carpenters and draftsmen can design houses."

"It's the same with landscape architects. They nothing but glorified gardeners," Dick Kawasaki says.

"That's right. We form our own clubs to keep out the riff-raffs," Lenny says.

"Shit, they pass only eight to ten percent every year," I say.

"There you go," Lenny says.

I get so antsy waiting for the test results. I can only relax on the board. I get there at 6:30, stand all day, and go back after supper. Chuck is on his annual 4-month "study." He always takes off during the test. He's jinxing me, squeezing his ass I flunk.

I finish the floor plans for the Baldwin house and leave the tedious lettering for Ted Taketa, the junior draftsman. Ted comes in at 7:30, then Grace Chun, the secretary.

I'm so involved with drawing I hardly look up.

Then Grace runs up and shouts, "President Kennedy has been shot!"

We all go into Chuck's glassed-in inner office and turn on the radio.

Nothing's for sure except he's been shot. Then shot in the head. Who did the shooting? Where was Secret Service? Then it's confirmed, JFK is dead, and Lyndon Johnson is sworn in.

Suddenly I lose all my fight. David Baldwin's elevations can wait.

A Lee Harvey Oswald is arrested and 2 days later he's shot on national TV! We see it on our TV 10 hours later. The funeral too is tape-delayed. Until we get live TV, we're in the boondocks.

Then rumors fly. Jack Ruby killed Oswald to keep him from implicating others. Ruby has connections with the Mafia. The Dallas police are involved. Who else? Who has most to gain? LBJ? The Cubans? The Mafia? Nixon?

Then it's the second week in December and I'm all antsy again. *I cannot flunk site! Chuck will be all smiles. I'll be a peon the rest of my life, Chuck's houseboy.*

"Steve, phone call."

Probably David Baldwin, I think, *or another of Chuck's rich clients.*

"Hello."

"Mr. Steven T. Oyama?" a haole woman's voice says.

"Speaking."

"Congratulations, Mr. Oyama, you're now an architect."

"Thank you." I hesitate. *Somebody pulling my leg?*

"What are your credentials, Mr. Oyama?"

"I beg your pardon?"

"Where did you go to school? I need to put that in the program."

It's for real! Besides, she said "T" Oyama! "Ah, ah, grammar school, Liliuokalani in Pepelau, two years at Pepelau High, ah, ah, I got my high school equivalency diploma from McKinley in 1951, and my architecture training at the American School in Chicago."

"American School of Architecture?"

"No, it's a correspondence school in drafting."

"Oh."

"I've also been taking courses at University of Hawaii."

"Shall I put University of Hawaii then?"

"I was unclassified, I didn't graduate."

"Hmmm . . ."

"Who else passed?" I ask.

"Four of you. We'll be sending you the invitation for the reception."

"Thank you very much."

I dial home. "Hello, Ma, we made it! Yeah, I passed the exam! Yeah, she called me just now! Only four of us made it! Yeah! You there? Ma?" Then I hear a sob. She's choking, trying not to cry. "Yeah, thanks to you, Ma, we made it!"

Ted and Grace come and bubble congratulations.

I splurge and take the family to Lau Yee Chai in Waikiki and order the most expensive dishes. Afterward I show up at the Columbia and buy a round for the house. The guys joke, "Hey, that mean you not going drink with us no more?"

"Hey, I'm not a snob!"

The notice comes a few days later, then the invitation to the black-tie reception at the Pacific Club in January. The 3 others who passed all have master's degrees—a nisei, a Hawaiian, and a haole professor from Yale. Four out of 39 passed, and I'm the first noncollege man to pass in 15 years, the first ever high school dropout!

I buy Carol a mink stole to go with her formal. I feel like a monkey in my tux. Carol looks more scared than me when we walk into the exclusive Pacific Club. Once upon a time it was for haoles only. The large hall is standing room only, all the men in tuxes, 100 architects and their wives, about 1/3 are locals—Bula-heads, Pakés, and part-Hawaiians. Everybody is a college graduate except me. This is 100 times worse than the housewarming parties. *Damn Chuck, it's just like him to take off on his cruise.*

I see Mori making a beeline for us. I feel like ducking.

"Congratulations, Steve, you should be very proud." He extends a hand.

"Oh, thanks, Andrew. This is my wife, Carol."

He clasps my hand firmly and turns to Carol. "You should be very proud of him, Carol. Steve's a natural." He turns to me. "I've got some work for you."

Wow! What a turnaround!

He escorts us to a haole couple. "This is Steve and Carol Oyama. Steve's one of the best designers I've seen in a long while."

I blush. "Andrew made me a better architect by flunking me so much."

He squires us around to other architects.

I get another surprise when I sit down at the dais and pick up my program. All 4 of us are listed without credentials! They didn't want to embarrass me!

I write to my siblings in yellow legal pad with 5 carbon copies:

I am now an architect, not A.I.A. until my certificate comes from Washington, D.C. I'm the 1st high school dropout to pass the test. The 1st non-college man in 15 years! They passed only 4 out of 39! Georgie, go get your license. It's a 100-grand insurance. Here's more low-downs:

(1) Rich old widows—collect 1st. One past 80 said "Take it out on me."

(2) Lawyers—no class

(3) Doctors—they deal with death so much they're insurance poor, no money

(4) Dentists—good clients

(5) Businessmen—the best. They make fast buck and not afraid to spend

(6) Contractors—next best . . .

The contractors and manufacturer reps bring cases of J&B and Chivas Regal to the house. They throw me one party after another at all the teahouses in town. The contractors offer me $400 for use of my seal.

"Cannot. I wen bust my ass for my AIA suffix. I don't wanna lose it over chicken feed."

Danny Lowe, who's now head of the state Boxing Commission, wants to do an article on me in the sports section of the *Star-Bulletin*, captioned "All Fighters Are Not Bums."

"Naw, not yet. Wait till I make my reputation. I don't wanna be pegged as a 'pug' before I start."

"You know, you should take a Dale Carnegie course," Carol says. "You're too blunt."

So I enroll in "How to Win Friends and Influence People" 2 nights a week. We practice making speeches. It's a lot of B.S., like putting facades over natural wood. But whenever I get up to talk, my voice backs up my nose.

"You're swallowing your voice. Breathe with your diaphragm. Right here," old Mrs. Wright says, pushing in my gut. "Now keep your throat clear and throw out your voice from your chest."

"You're talking too fast," she keeps saying. "We can't understand you."

I pretend I'm Jim Horne and slow down my rapid-fire pidgin delivery. I can do prepared speeches okay, but the extemporaneous stuff floors me. I need barely move my mouth in speaking pidgin or Japanese. But now I have to stick out my tongue, spray spit, make chicken ass, or open real wide till my cheeks hurt.

"Very good!" Mrs. Wright says. "But you have to keep practicing."

"How come you making faces li'dat?" Danny says at supper.

"I'm learning to talk from both sides of my mouth."

"Why, in heaven's name?" schoolmarmish Marcia asks.

"I want to go into politics. HAW-HAW!"

27

A Certificate to Starvation

When Chuck returns from his 4-month cruise, I ask for a meeting. He's real happy when I tell him I'd like to stay with him. But I want a percentage now, not a salary.

He doodles and says, "How does seventy/thirty sound?" He pushes over his doodling to me. It reads, 'Charles B. Ames and Assoc., AIA.'

"What about putting my name there instead of associate?" I ask.

"Well, I bring in all the jobs. My clients come because of my name, my identity. Who is Steve Oyama? Remember Jim Horne? He had no identity."

Jim didn't last 6 months when he went on his own.

"Lemme think about it," I say.

I phone Ichiro Kono. He's a big wheel in the Republican party. All successful nisei politicians in his day were Republicans. He invited Carol and me to their family reunion soon after Ann married his brother. I felt I was back at the housewarming parties. They had 2 doctors, 2 lawyers, and 2 sisters were teachers. But Ichiro was a polite host, though bossy like all number-one sons.

"You should take it," Ichiro says right away. "Mr. Ames has all the connections. Besides, you don't even have a college degree. Who's going to come to you? You have no identity. What did you design?"

"Barbara Hutton's house in Mexico."

"Does it say, 'Architect: Steven Oyama?' No, it says, 'Architect: Charles Ames.' Even if you designed it, it's his, not yours."

"I also did Dr. Hamada's house, Jim Kawahara's, Anna Hagen's, Bob Agena—"

"Does it say, 'Steve Oyama.' No, it says, 'Charles Ames.' Do you know the first thing I looked at on the applications when I ran the attorney general's office?

"Yeah? What?"

"Was it Harvard, Yale, or Podunk. You don't even have Podunk. Who's gonna come to you?"

"But Ames needs me more than I need him. He's sixty-five and he never been on the board for over sixteen years."

"So how old are you?"

"Forty-four."

"You're starting out at forty-four with not even Podunk, no identity, and no connections. How do you expect to survive?"

"I know the business inside out."

"So what? Who knows that? What are your credentials?"

"Thanks anyway."

"Have you done a presentation to a group of haoles?"

"Yeah."

"Who?"

"The Dillinghams, the Hagens."

"I mean a group in a formal presentation. You cannot talk 'da kine' to them, you know. You—"

"Thanks, Ichiro, I'll think about it," I say, and hang up.

Damn Uncle Tom! They're all ass-kissers, these older nisei politicians! That's how they got ahead! And now they spout the haole party line!

Peter Doi is like that, I think afterward, *and the guys at the mill. They're so jealous, they try to nail you down. They don't wanna see you climb past them. At least now I'm not taking it personally. It's them, not me! They cannot take away my AIA!*

I complain to Carol, "Bulaheads are such snobs. They got a pecking order for everything."

"Mr. Ames and the *hakujin*s are bigger snobs," Carol counters.

"But Bulaheads are meticulous."

I ask my drinking buddies that night. Dick Kawasaki says, "All the architects starving, but Ames, the society architect, goes on and on."

"What about you, you're not starving," I say.

"He gets all the government jobs, that's why," Lenny Imai says.

"How come you don't get government jobs," I ask Lenny.

"I don't contribute, that's why."

"It's not contribution, it's investment," Dick says.

"So how come you don't invest?" I ask Lenny.

"He rather starve," Dick says.

"Than produce bland architecture," Lenny says.

"What do you think I should do?" I ask Lenny.

"It depends. You wanna keep working for your colonial paymaster or you wanna strike out on your own?"

"And strike out?" Dick says.

I cannot accept the offer, I tell Chuck. He says he'll revise it to "Charles B. Ames and Steven T. Oyama" at the same 70/30.

"Let me think about it."

"But you *said* that's what you wanted." His face turns red.

"I have to talk to some people." I forget Dale Carnegie and my voice goes up my nose when I feel apologetic.

I call Ichiro Kono's office again and ask for an appointment with his younger brother, who's also a lawyer. All appointments have to go through Ichiro, the secretary says. I call Ichiro's nephew, a young kid just out of law school. Alvin Sawada is *hapa;* his mother is Hawaiian. His father is Doc Sawada's brother. Alvin works for another firm.

"Don't take it," he says. "In a lawsuit you're liable fifty/fifty, not seventy/thirty."

"You think I ought to string along with Chuck for the next couple of years? It's a twenty-G guarantee. I don't know how much I can make on my own. I can keep doing residentials. You never get rich on them, but it'll be a start while I build my identity."

"The house is paid for. We've got three thousand dollars in the bank," Carol says.

"Yeah, but what if I cannot scare up clients?"

"We'll all have to tighten our belts."

"It's not as if he's hiring me. We'll be partners."

"At seventy-thirty? Does that mean we'll be invited to the housewarmings?"

"What if we starve?"

"We'll all pitch in."

The next day I tell myself, *Take the jump, I'm way ahead of the pack.* I know labor and materials costs. I can estimate costs per square foot while sketching. And I know every phase, I can protect the client in scheduling and everything.

Andy Mori invites me to lunch. "Your first job is to satisfy the client. Clients like me because I meet their budgets," he says, but the job he has for me is a cheap 40-G remodeling of a residential.

According to AIA ethics architects cannot compete with each other—you cannot take over a job unless the first architect is paid off and dismissed. What I'll do is flood Honolulu with prelims. If anybody uses one of them, I'll turn him in and charge the client. That'll keep me going if . . . I keep thinking of Jim Horne, who didn't last 6 months. But he was a plodder and a gin mill.

One day I'm all for accepting 70/30, the next day I'm pissing mad at Ames for taking me so cheap. It's a generation thing— the older guys say, "Take it"; the younger guys say, "No be one sucker. The plantation days are over." These young guys are not scared to take out big loans. "You never get rich on pay-as-you go," they say.

"Can we talk?" I say the next time Ames comes in.

"I'll take Charles B. Ames and Steven T. Oyama, seventy-thirty," I say, "provided I have some say in the expenses. I don't think it's fair when you take off four months a year."

"It's for study."

"Study, vacation, I end up running the office."

He looks away. His face is more puffed. *Bourbon fat.*

"I tell you what, I'll accept your four-month 'study' if it's sixty-forty."

He jumps up like a jack-in-the-box and runs. I watch him scoot out of the outer office and slam the door.

Well, fuck you too!

"I'm going on my own," I tell him the next time. I'll split the rent, office expense, and salaries of the secretary and the draftsman if he lets me use the office. Anything we do together will be 50/50.

He nods. No handshake.

Alvin Sawada helps me form a corporation with Carol, "Steven T. Oyama and Associates, Inc."

"How much I owe you?"

"Forget it. Calabash," he says.

I get butterflies like the first time I climbed into the ring. *All I doing now is climbing out of the plantation! But I got 4 kids. . . .* When Georgie started his drafting business he had 2 rentals to fall back on. Now he has 4 and works out of his home and has only 1 kid. "You never win by playing it safe," Kiyo writes, but he has no kids and can play the horses all he wants. All I have is $3,000 in the bank. A month goes by. I go to Pepelau to talk to Alan Freeland, who owns the Frontier Theatre and some land. With the Kaanapali tourist resort coming up, he can make a fortune developing his land. But he's already committed to Mori. Who else do I know who's rich?

In the second month Erica Hagen calls me. She and her sister were sole heirs of Hackfeld and Co., which was seized by the government during World War I as German property. The company was resold and renamed American Factors, and the sisters got big settlements.

"Steve, I want you to come to the house," she says. "I don't want Uncle Chuck to touch it. I want to keep it under two hundred thousand."

"Erica, Chuck and I are not together any more. I've set up my own practice."

"You can still do it. I like what you did for Anna."

"But I have to talk to Chuck first. I'll do it if he doesn't want it."

"Do you have to?"

"Yes. I'm not working for him any more."

"But he'll make it four hundred thousand."

"But I have to." *No way Ames will turn it down.*

"Can't you do it by yourself?"

"Why don't you talk to Chuck? If he can't, I'll be happy to do it."

"Why did you split with him? Did you have a row?"

"No, I finally got my license. I want to establish my own identity."

"It's too bad!" She sounds angry.

There goes 30 percent of $20,000, an easy 6 Gs! She and her sister always pay promptly too! But shit! Chuck gets 14 Gs without lifting a finger! It was MY design for her sister that brought in the job! I might as well have stayed on the plantation if I'm going to take shit like that!

I need to learn to golf, meet people, hang around with politicians, contribute to their campaigns. I call Tommy Hida, who's a supervisor in Maui County, and an old friend from my boxing days. "Yeah, Steve, we'll keep you in mind," he says.

The younger nisei and *sansei* architects are grabbing up most of the state contracts. Half of the state legislators are niseis. Who do I know? Ben Moriyama, Carol's classmate at Pepelau High, is a 100th vet and one of Gov. Burns' inner circle. Another veteran, Yoshio Nishikawa, is a friend from my boxing days and senator from Maui. I wouldn't have known them except for my boxing. They all came to see me fight. But I cannot just call them. I remember my classmate, Kaba, when he set up his dental practice. He sat around for 2 months, waiting for patients. He called all his friends but they all had their own dentists.

Most nights I'm at the Columbia. After several drinks Dick Kawasaki repeats his broken record, "All the architects starving but Ames, the society architect, goes on and on . . ."

Maybe I should have taken 70/30. Nah . . . I did the right thing. I oughta thank Chuck for kicking me out of my plantation mentality.

About the Author

MILTON ATSUSHI MURAYAMA was born in Lahaina, Maui, and grew up in Lahaina and Puukolii, a sugar plantation company town that no longer exists. He attended Lahainaluna High School. During World War II he trained at the Military Intelligence Language School at Camp Savage, Minnesota, and served as an interpreter in India and China. Murayama received a BA in English from the University of Hawaii and an MA in Chinese and Japanese from Columbia University. He has worked at various jobs and has lived in Minneapolis, New York, and Washington, D.C. He presently resides in San Francisco with his wife. Murayama is the author of *All I Asking for Is My Body* and has written a play based on it. *Plantation Boy, Five Years on a Rock,* and *All I Asking* form the first three parts of a tetralogy.